MURDER IN SHADES OF BLUE AND GREEN

DS Charlie Rees Book 1

RIPLEY HAYES

A night at the Rainbow
SUNDAY EVENING

Exclusive: Sun, sex and murder! Gay cop's holiday hook-up ends in murder trial.

Charlie Rees was frustrated, miserable, and well on the way to being drunk. Worse, he had no one to blame but himself. *Bringing the service into disrepute.* The judge said he hadn't been on trial, but he'd been tried by the media and been found guilty. All he'd done was take a week's holiday in Lanzarote because his bosses said he was burned out. A night in a gay bar had landed him in the middle of a nasty murder followed by a media feeding frenzy with him as their prey. That he'd solved the case mattered not at all. What mattered was that his name was splattered all over social media, as if he had any control over that.

He'd been lucky not to be back in uniform facing years of breaking up fights outside licensed premises, operating speed cameras in remote villages, and maybe sitting in a patrol car waiting for sheep rustlers to turn up, or not. Instead, he'd been offered a last chance to redeem himself, by transferring away from his friends and colleagues and into the middle of another media storm in the college town of Llanfair. The price of failure would be the opportunity to resign and keep his pension. Like he cared about a pension. He was barely thirty. So, here he was, halfway between his old life and the new one, drinking alone in a bar nowhere near either place, hoping no one here knew who he was.

His mother's voice was the soundtrack to his thoughts: *I hardly dare show my face in the town. I didn't raise you to behave like this. Your face all over the papers. No self-discipline, that's always been your trouble, Charles.*

He finished his beer and asked for another.

The bar was getting darker and the music louder as it got later. Men were dancing, making out, and occasionally disappearing, returning with swollen lips and blissed-out expressions. The bar staff—all good-looking men—had stripped down to tiny tank tops.

"Let me get that," a voice said from by his left shoulder. Charlie looked round. A big man with a black beard, was frowning in his direction. Charlie was sitting on a bar stool, and the man towered over him. He wore a red checked flannel shirt over a white T-shirt, sleeves rolled up to show his tats. By any measure, the guy was hot, but Charlie wasn't interested. He was too busy beating himself up about the man who'd lied in Lanzarote. The man he could still lose his job over, because he, Charlie, was too stupid to…well, just too stupid.

"I'm fine," Charlie said.

"You're obviously not," the man replied. "Want to talk about it?"

"That would be no." Charlie wished the man would go away. His willingness to make nice, even to obviously nice guys, had deserted him several drinks ago. He shouldn't be here. Yet another failure of judgement.

"Then I'll buy you a drink and wait here in case you change your mind. I'm Tom, by the way."

"Not going to happen." Charlie turned away, but not before he saw the man signal to the bartender.

"There's a drag show later," Charlie heard the man say. He said nothing. "She's really good,"

"I don't like drag," Charlie said, without turning. He did, but jeez, would this guy not take a hint?

"You'll like this," Tom said. "She's a friend of mine. I promise she'll cheer you up."

"I told you, I'm fine."

"You are one terrible liar. And you are headed for a hell of a hangover."

This time Charlie did turn round. "What is with you? Recruiting for a temperance society?"

Tom held up his glass, which held something dark. Rum? "No temperance here. But a lot of experience with feeling crap and having hangovers."

"Social worker then? Or just a general do-gooder?" Charlie sighed, picking at the label on his beer bottle rather than looking at the big man. Who was attractive, and had a soft, deep, voice Charlie liked.

There was no sign that he'd noticed Charlie's irritation. He leaned against the bar and smiled. "I saw a seriously hot guy looking miserable, and thought I'd buy him a drink. Maybe chat him up a little. So shoot me."

"Seriously hot guy?" Charlie snorted.

"I'm looking at him."

Charlie snorted again and folded his arms. He wanted to like the compliment, but he knew what he was. Skinny, pale, not very tall. He worked out, but it didn't show. His mother said he had an interesting face, by which she meant he wasn't good-looking. He was used to it.

"Look," he said, "I appreciate your making the effort, but

I'm really not worth it. Enjoy the drag act." He stood up, realising too late that he'd had too much to drink. Now he was going to make a dick of himself by stumbling out of the bar, and probably throwing up in the gutter. The room swam around him, and he gripped the dark wood of the bar for stability in a tilting world. Fuck.

He felt a strong arm round his waist and smelled rum and some kind of cologne that reminded him of childhood. He leaned against the plaid shirt, because there was no choice. It was that or fall over.

"Let's get you out of here."

The fresh air hit Charlie like a bucket of ice on his head, clearing it. He was still drunk, but not falling-over-drunk any more.

"Thanks," he said. "I can take it from here."

The arm stayed round him. He realised the cologne was Old Spice. His mother had dutifully bought bottles for his father and both his grandfathers every Christmas. He hadn't known you could still get it. Maybe this guy had raided his own grandfather's stash. Maybe he also had a mother who thought it was a classic.

"Can I call someone to pick you up? Or a cab to take you home?" Tom's voice was patient and sounded as if the questions had been asked more than once.

"There's no one." It was true. He had meant to stop at the bar, have one drink and then drive to Llanfair and find a place to stay. He'd moved out of his flat, and all his possessions were in the car. Looked like he would be sleeping in the car, too. If he could remember where he'd parked it. "Long story. Just a bit of temporary homelessness." The word *homelessness* came out all wrong and he tried it again. "But I'll be fine. Sleep on the beach."

The arm tightened round him. "It's October. And someone will call the police if they see you stumbling along in this state."

4

Charlie said what he almost never said to civilians. "I am the fucking police." Then he pulled himself free from the lumberjack grip and half-ran, half-fell in what he hoped was the right direction for his car.

2

Not in love with my car

Charlie's first thought on waking was that he needed to pee so urgently that he would have done it in a jam jar if he had one. His second thought was that he was probably going to wet himself because all his limbs had seized up. Sand had blown across the road from the dunes beyond the hedge, and it crunched under his feet as he levered himself painfully out of the car. Seagulls screamed overhead, white and prehistoric against the early morning sky.

He staggered, stiff-legged closer to the hedge, looked up and down the road for passers-by, and relieved himself with a groan. That done, every other pain and discomfort piled in to fill its place. He was stiff and sore from sleeping in the cramped driver's seat of his car. He was also freezing, with random wet patches on his clothes from the condensation dripping down every piece of glass. During the night, his brain had shrunk inside his skull. His head pounded. And he stank.

Thankfully he had parked next to a tall hedge by a parade of shops, built, he guessed, as cheaply as possible in the 1970s and badly maintained ever since. Rust marks dripped down the concrete facades between the shops. Each business had adopted its own style of signage and the windows were different sizes. With a bit of effort, it could have been attractive. As it was, Charlie imagined the locals were just happy to have the shops. There was a Spar, a Bargain Booze, a fish and chip shop, a vet, a hairdresser and a bookmaker, with diagonal parking spaces painted in front of them, all empty. On either side, small, neat bungalows stretched off into the distance. The town proper was only half a mile away, but he had wanted somewhere quiet to park.

The clock on the dashboard read seven-oh-five, which meant that shops would (hopefully) open soon. Good news that he could get coffee, bad news that people would see (and smell) him. So, he might as well get moving and find a quiet lay-by where he could change his clothes, brush his teeth and wield the deodorant. No part of him wanted to arrive in Llanfair, but he'd said yes to the job, and he was damned if he was going to appear looking like someone who'd slept in his car. There was a bottle of water on the floor underneath the passenger seat. Getting it out was agony, but he drank until his stomach sloshed. *Rehydrate*, he told his body, and forced another mouthful of water down.

There were painkillers in one of his suitcases in the boot, and God knew, he needed them. He dragged himself out of the car again. Which was when he saw the flat tyre--correction, flat tyres, plural. Both the wheels on the passenger side were resting on their rims, the tyres a puddle of black rubber on the road underneath. Charlie laid his forearms on the top of the car, put his head on them, closed his eyes and gave himself up to welcome darkness, until he heard a voice say, "You alright there, son?"

He straightened up to see an elderly man in heavy trousers and a navy-blue duffle coat, with a head of fine white hair, watching him with bright blue eyes. A small white dog, the nearest thing Charlie had seen to a string mop, sat at the man's feet.

The man indicated the tyres with the hand not holding the dog's lead. "Kids. It's the latest craze. It'll pass, but until then, I've been hearing new swear words most mornings. And I did forty years in the Merchant Navy." The man shook his head. "Do you want the garage number?"

Charlie considered. He could get the tyres fixed here and be late for his first day. Or he could turn up on time, smelling of last night's booze, with his car and all his possessions on the back of a police tow truck. The choice was impossible. The indecision must have shown on his face.

"If it's the money, son, they don't replace the tyres, just blow them up and pump them full of some stuff to keep you going."

"It's not that, Charlie said. "I'm supposed to be in Llanfair for nine, to start a new job. Believe it or not, I'm a police officer."

The man's face hardened, frown lines appearing above his eyebrows. "Llanfair police don't have a great reputation," the man said.

"My job is to sort it out," Charlie said. "Which is why I don't want to be late."

The man shook his head, and then held his hand out. "Hayden James," he said. "Seaman, retired."

"Detective Sergeant Charlie Rees." Charlie shook the outstretched hand, wondering what on Earth was happening.

"You've got an honest face, Charlie Rees. That's my place, up there." He pointed to some windows over the parade of shops. You look like you could use a cup of tea and a bacon sandwich. Come back with me and Bosun here." The little dog wagged his tail at the sound of his name. "Phone the garage, and stay in the warm, until they get here. They won't be long. As for that shower in Llanfair, make 'em wait."

Charlie looked down at his crumpled jeans and even more crumpled hoodie. The evidence of his night in the car was plain to see from his grubby clothes, his unshaven chin and the blanket hanging over the steering wheel. Hayden James must be very discerning to see anything but disaster in Charlie's face.

"Are you sure?" Because if he was, Charlie wasn't going to refuse.

Hayden James patted Charlie on the arm. "Wouldn't offer if I didn't mean it. Bring a change of clothes and your shaving kit if you like."

Truly, the man was an angel.

THE VIEW from the flat above the shops was astounding. From the outside, the entrance looked as tatty as the shops, but inside, it was flooded with light and filled with the sight of the sea. By the biggest window, Hayden had set up a tele-scope on a tripod, a beautiful brass instrument that was clearly in regular use. The window drew Charlie, his dirty clothes and unshaven chin forgotten in the face of the drama in front of his eyes. From here, the viewer could see over the hedge to the dunes with their topknots of grey-green marram grass, moving softly in the breeze. Then the beach itself, huge and yellow at low tide. And beyond it all, the rest-less sea. The sun was shining close to the beach, speckling the water with flecks of gold, but low white clouds lay on the horizon.

"On a clear day, you can see the Wirral," Hayden said. "Would you believe the woman I bought it from had net curtains? I've only been here a couple of years, but they'll have to carry me out in a box." He waved his hand to encom-pass the view. "But she left me a painting of the sea. Funny woman. Went to live near family somewhere near Manchester."

The painting was on the opposite wall. It was nothing like the view from the window. It showed a small boat being tossed around on towering waves.

"I prefer the view from your window. It's magnificent," said Charlie. "I could sit here all day."

"That's why I have a dog. They insist you get up and out." Hayden peered at the painting. "The sea isn't always as pretty as it is today. I'd like to meet whoever did this, because this is just as realistic as that beach out there. Dunno who the artist was. All it says on the back is number four, in Roman numerals like, and I often wonder if the other three are as good."

Charlie noticed that Bosun had curled up in his basket with half an eye open, just in case. He had no interest in the view, or the painting, just in the possibilities of the opening fridge door.

Hayden showed Charlie the spotlessly clean bathroom and told him he had ten minutes to make himself respectable before breakfast would be on the table. When Charlie appeared, in a suit and clean shirt, his hair damp from the comb, teeth clean, and chin smooth, smelling of soap and a lemony aftershave, Hayden did a double take.

"Now you look like someone who can sort out those twisters in Llanfair," he said, then pointed to two padded wooden armchairs facing the window. There was a small table between them, on which stood a Brown Betty teapot, cups and saucers, and two plates each with a thick bacon sandwich. There was a bottle of ketchup, and pieces of kitchen roll for napkins. Charlie took off his jacket and resolved to eat with care.

"This is wonderful, thank you," he said.

"There's not enough kindness offered any more," Hayden said. "All you've cost me are two slices of bread, two rashers of bacon, and thruppence to ring the garage. In exchange, I've had some company, and the feeling of virtue will last all day. I can tell everyone that I know the man who is going to sort Llanfair out. Cheap at twice the price." He twinkled his eyes at Charlie, who laughed, at ease for the first time in days.

"The garage is sending someone," Hayden went on. "They'll be here in about twenty minutes, so sup up."

Charlie duly supped and ate his sandwich without ketchup in case of drips on his clean clothes.

"If the garage people are quick, I'll still be there by nine," he said. "I don't usually sleep in my car. I was planning to get there last night and find somewhere to stay, only I had one too many drinks."

"I know," Hayden said with a wink. "I saw you roll back after midnight. I always have a look out of the window when I get up in the night." He shrugged. "Old man's problems." There was a pause, and Charlie saw a faint flush on Hayden's cheeks.

"I have a friend," he said, hesitantly. "A lady friend, Dilys. She lives in Llanfair and rents out a couple of rooms. For travelling workers, like, not tourists. Nothing fancy, but clean, and she's a good cook. She knows everyone in the town. Maybe that might be useful, or maybe I should keep my big nose out."

"Actually," Charlie said, "that would be perfect. I'd love her number."

Hayden's smile was back, and his eyes twinkled again. "I'll do better than that. I'll ring her. Always good to have an excuse." The blush was back, but Charlie didn't think it meant the same as before.

Out of the window, Charlie saw a van arrive, and pull up next to his car. A man in overalls got out and peered at the flat tires.

"They're here," Charlie said, gathering up his dirty clothes and washbag.

Hayden ushered him out, promising to come down as soon as he'd spoken to Dilys.

· · ·

"Keeping us in business, the kids round here," the mechanic said. He had already begun to jack up the car to fill the tyre with goopy stuff to stop any punctures. "They don't make holes, just let the air out, so this is a just-in-case." Charlie nodded. The police used it routinely. The mechanic was quick and efficient and had a card reader for the modest bill. As he got back into his van, Hayden arrived with a piece of paper.

"I hope you weren't just being polite, because I've booked you into Dilys's place for tonight. She's got room if you want to stay longer. Number, and address." He handed the paper over.

Charlie put it carefully in his wallet. "I wasn't being polite. I can't thank you enough for all your help, but I'd better go."

"Make them wait," Hayden almost growled.

I daren't.

As he drove away, with a wave to Hayden, Charlie thought about the kindness of strangers. A man he had known for an hour thought he was the man to "sort out those twisters in Llanfair."

OK. I'll give it my best shot. Only it's not the twisters themselves I have to deal with. It's the mess they left behind.

3

Aftermath
MONDAY 9AM

From the North Wales Courier and Post

The Llanfair College of Art scandal continued today with the suspension of the town's most senior police officers. They have been named locally as Inspector Nigel Harrington-Bowen and Sergeant Jared Brody. The Courier and Post understands that two other officers have been transferred to Colwyn Bay. The enquiry into the scandal is being led by Detective Superintendent Maldwyn Kent of Clwyd Police. When contacted, he had no comment to make.

From the Action for Women website

The parents of art student Matilda Everard have demanded action from Llanfair College of Art as their daughter recovers in hospital after a suicide attempt.

"Matilda reported that she'd been assaulted in the town, and no one listened," Jane Everard, Matilda's mother, told our reporter. "The college has a duty of care to their students. Instead, they colluded with the police in covering up."

A Clwyd Police spokesman said that the investigation was ongoing

"I NEED you to sort out this report of two missing students. As far as I can tell, nothing to do with the assaults on young women." Mal Kent had told Charlie. "The college says it's not a big deal, students disappear and come back all the time, but I've had one of the dads on the phone, worried sick. He says Rico, that's his son, contacts home every day without fail and they haven't heard from him for over a week. His dad also says Rico hasn't spent any money for a week either; they have access to his account online."

"How old?" Charlie asked.

"Nineteen. From the States. His parents live there. So is the other one, Kaylan, an American, I mean. But we only found out about him because they both missed the same trip yesterday. It could be a storm in a teacup, or it could be serious."

"What have the locals done to find them? Or the people at the college?"

Kent sighed and lined up his pen and notebook until they were exactly parallel with the sleek laptop which was the only other thing on his desk.

"You know what state the local police are in, and the college is in worse chaos than the police. The governing body of the college has had to bring some bloke back from his sabbatical in New York to take over as Principal, because Sir John Singer has, I quote, *stepped aside*. The new bloke is a Dr Tomos Pennant. So go and find out if Rico and Kaylan are actually missing, and if they are, find them. We can't afford for anything else to go wrong in Llanfair."

"What about the assaults? Charlie asked. "Am I looking into those too?"

"If you trip over any evidence, share it. But the whole question of the assaults has become so political that I don't know if it will ever be resolved. Evidence. That's what we need. There are already enough theories to sink a ship."

No pressure, then.

It wasn't far from the north Wales coast to the college town of Llanfair. The road followed the course of the river valley, flat in the valley bottom with views of the mountains of Eryri—Snowdonia—on the right. As he drove, he could see the river estuary as it meandered towards the sea. The sun sparkled on the water, blue and gold, as it had from Hayden's windows. The river narrowed as he went south away from the sea, but the valley was wide, with roads and railway clinging to the edges of steep slopes. Across the valley, the land rose steeply, the lower slopes of the mountains covered with trees. There could have been a sign: Glacier Was Here. No roads crossed the valley, because the only bridges were at the coast and forty miles further south at Llanfair. He was only an hour and a half away from his old home in Melin Tywyll, but it felt like another world.

Only the sheep were the same—looking bleached against grass shining emerald in the sun. The leaves had begun to turn on the higher ground, gold and copper mixed in with the remaining greens.

The hangover headache lurked in the back of Charlie's skull, and the night in the car was still all too present in sore limbs and joints in need of oil. But the churning in his gut, and the pain in his chest pushed those minor aches and pains to one side. Nerves made every breath hurt, and the closer he got, the worse he felt.

There had been nine police officers, all in uniform, at the Llanfair station—a lot for such a small town. But the famous art college carried weight amongst the powers-that-be in Clwyd Police. Of the nine, five were left: four women constables, and the trainee who had blown the whistle.

"It doesn't mean they weren't involved. It's just less likely," Kent had said.

Everyone else had either resigned or been suspended. That was the police, and Charlie understood how the police worked, or in this case, didn't. But there was the college too, and that was new territory. According to his information, the college management had only acted after one of the victims had attempted suicide. Even as the principal "stepped aside" which seemed to be code for "will be keeping a low profile until the heat dies down", the official statements denied any wrongdoing.

As people had been saying since Watergate: *it's not so much the crime as the cover-up that causes the trouble...*

THE LLANFAIR POLICE station was on the edge of the town. It was an Arts and Crafts style building of dark grey slate with a gabled frontage. Blue paint peeled from the window frames and the wooden noticeboard fixed to the outside wall. The windows were small, and even on this bright day, Charlie saw lights on behind them all. He thought he caught sight of a face peering out, but it disappeared before he could be sure he hadn't imagined it. There was a small car park behind the building, and he parked next to a patrol car, got out, checked he had his ID, his phone and wallet, and locked the car. His legs felt as if they belonged to another man, his headache was back with full force, and he wanted to throw up. Missing students, he told himself. The town is entitled to competent policing, and that's why I'm here.

As he walked around the building, his phone vibrated with a text.

Supt Kent: *Good luck. I am sure you will do a thoroughly professional job.*

I'm glad one of us is, because I'm not sure of anything.

Charlie slipped the phone back into his pocket. It was a minute before nine. He took a deep breath and pushed at the door to the police station, painted in the same sun-whitened blue paint that was peeling from the windows and notice board.

It didn't open.

Could this morning get any worse?

Apparently, it could.

"They don't let anyone inside anymore. You have to ring up. The number's on the notice," a woman's voice said behind him. Then a black dog, the size of a small horse, or so it seemed, leapt at him, almost knocking him down. The dog licked Charlie's face with enthusiasm and delight, as the woman pulled ineffectively at its lead.

"Coco! Get down! I'm so sorry. Coco! No! Come here!"

Huge paws raked down the front of Charlie's suit, tearing the cloth and leaving smears of mud. The dog panted and danced on its hind legs at the end of its lead, desperate for another go.

The woman held on for grim death. She and Charlie looked at each other, and at the dog. The woman's clothes were also torn and muddy.

"I know," she said. "I do know. He's out of control. He's not mine, but his owner's in hospital." She looked pleadingly at Charlie, and he saw tears in her eyes.

"Better not take him into town," Charlie said. He was pissed off at the wreck of his suit but couldn't help sympathising with the woman.

"You're right. I'm not. Just to my car, there." She pointed to a battered white Corsa. "I don't know what to say. Send me the bill for the mending and cleaning."

"How many dry-cleaning bills have you had?"

"Three. And it's only been a week."

Charlie felt his anxiety lift, leaving calmness in its place. Because there was now nothing he could do to appear professional. He smiled at the woman. "Let me help you get him back to your car," he said. "Then I suggest you go home and google dog trainers."

Once in the car, the dog settled as if assaulting passers-by would never occur to him.

"Thank you," the woman said. "Now, your suit …"

Charlie shrugged. "Don't worry, I've got others." He turned back to the police station with a wave.

When he got there, he rang the number on the notice board.

No one answered.

There were lights on, a patrol car in the car park and he was sure he had seen a face in one of the windows. He walked back around to the car park, stood next to his own car, then banged very hard with his fist on the roof of the marked patrol car.

The alarm was deafening. But it worked. An inconspicuous door at the back of the station building opened and a woman in uniform appeared. She didn't move from the doorway, just shouted for him to get away from the cars. Charlie flipped his warrant card folder open and held it up as he walked towards the door. He was by the door when the alarm stopped, the silence as shocking as the noise had been.

"DS Rees," Charlie said. "You should be expecting me."

The police officer looked at his torn and muddy suit and blushed crimson. "Yes, Sarge," she said. She didn't move. She stood as if frozen to the ground, her arms stiff by her side. She must have been about thirty, Charlie thought, taking in the bleached blonde hair tied back in a ponytail, with a fringe caressing the top of perfectly groomed eyebrows. Make-up gave her face a flawless skin, and she was girl-next-door pretty. But fear came off her in waves. The hands by her sides were clenched into fists, and as he watched, the colour drained from her face leaving it ashen. He smelled sweat beneath the scent of deodorant and body lotion.

"Constable?" Charlie asked. "Were you planning to let me in?"

"Yes, Sarge." Her voice squeaked, then cracked. "PC Margaret Jellicoe, Sarge." She moved, visibly un-sticking her feet from the ground, and moving backwards into a clean but tatty passageway.

There was a loud hammering from the front of the building. Jellicoe flinched. The hammering continued.

"We… we've been told to keep the door locked," she said.

"Really? By whom?" Charlie asked.

"Superintendent Kent."

Charlie weighed the statement and found it wanting. "I don't think so, constable. You'll have to do better than that."

Jellicoe looked around wildly. "He did, Sarge."

Charlie heard the crunch of feet on gravel. "Hello, hello," said a voice from behind him. He turned to see a very tall, very broad man, dressed in a tan suit that must have been made for him, because no off-the-peg suit would be large enough. As Charlie had done five minutes before, he held up a warrant card. "DC Eddy Edwards, seconded from Wrexham," he said. "What's going on?"

"DS Charlie Rees," Charlie said.

"DS…?" Edwards' eyebrows rose as he looked Charlie up and down, taking in the torn and muddy suit.

"Come in and close the door," Charlie said, without acknowledging the look. "Constable Jellicoe here is going to explain what's happening. I think coffee would help, though. Where can we brew up? Constable?"

"Through here," she said, and led the way to a break room overlooking the car park. The light was on, showing a fridge with a kettle on top next to a battered stainless steel sink. A shelf above held a disparate selection of mugs, a jar of the cheapest instant coffee, a bag of sugar and a box of tea bags. Teaspoons drained next to the sink. There were two coffee tables, each with a couple of battered chairs, padded and upholstered in blue to match the carpet, foam showing through on the corners.

Charlie filled the kettle and took three mugs from the shelf. He turned to Jellicoe. "Is there anyone else here?"

"No, sir. Not in the morning. There are only five of us, sir."

"Seven now," Charlie said. "Who wants what?"

He made the drinks strong and black for him, weak and black for Jellicoe, and builders' tea with lots of sugar for Eddy. He handed them out, indicated the seats and sat down. Across the table, Jellicoe wrapped her fingers around the hot mug, and stared down at the steam rising from the coffee.

Edwards overwhelmed his chair. He was in his late twenties or early thirties, with the face and body of someone who had played a lot of rugby, but from the softening around the middle, not recently. His shoulders looked like battering rams, with thighs to match, very short hair and features that had spent too long face down on a muddy field. Charlie imagined him as the kind of player who is slow to start, and then unstoppable. He was at least six foot four, maybe taller, and made Charlie feel decidedly petite in comparison. He was the second person to have that effect in two days, and he couldn't decide if he liked it. He'd quite liked it in from the hot guy in the Rainbow, less so at work.

"Right then," he said. "Let's see if we can get this show on the road."

4

Internationally renowned art college
MONDAY 9.30AM

From: Listen to Women's Stories, a podcast about sexual violence

Trigger Warning: explicit account of sexual exposure/flashing. Account of threatening behaviour.

Art student Jordie Miles spoke to WS about her experience in Llanfair.

WS: Thank you for speaking to us Jordie. Why have you decided to do this?

JM: I know that the listeners to this podcast will believe my story. When I reported it to the police, they weren't interested. When I reported it to the college, I wasn't believed. But it happened, and it was horrible. Women need to know what's going on in Llanfair. It's important.

WS: Would you tell listeners what happened to you? Take as long as you need to.

JM: Yes. It happened when I was in the library at the Art College. It's in the basement of the college, and it's full of nooks and crannies. I used to love the place... Sorry.

WS: Take your time.

JM: I was in the section with the DVDs. There are DVD players with headphones so we can watch movies, documentaries, videos of exhibi-

*tions and so on. I was watching a documentary about David Hockney. I
hadn't realised I was on my own in that part of the library …*

*WS: And I suppose you couldn't hear anything? Because of the
headphones?*

From: **Breaking News**

*A series of assaults on young women has created a state of terror in
the sleepy north Wales town of Llanfair. Internationally renowned Llanfair College of Art refused to comment on whether the victims were all
students at the college. A spokesperson for the college students' union said
that no action had been taken by college authorities or the local police.
"Women in the town are frightened," the spokesperson said.*

"I've had a report that two students from the college are missing, Rico Pepperdine and Kaylan Sully, both American,"
Charlie said. "That's why I'm here. The fallout from the
assaults is going to affect the way we work, but I'm not here to
investigate them. We aren't going to get co-operation from
anyone after what's happened, but we still have a job to do.
And that means opening the door to the public." He looked at
Jellicoe.

"We got an email from Superintendent Kent, sir, telling us
not to. Or to answer the phone."

"Let's give him a call and ask why he sent that, shall we?"
Charlie knew no such email had been sent. With only four officers available, opening hours would have to be restricted, but
one of the promises Clwyd Police had made was to maintain a
police presence in the town. Someone had sent the email in
Kent's name, or someone was lying abut receiving it. It was
another thing to be investigated, but not by him. PC Jellicoe
didn't look worried by the idea of calling Superintendent
Kent. She appeared to believe in the veracity of the email.

Charlie was prepared to accept that she hadn't sent it. Perhaps there was one person he could trust, at least. The others were wait and see. He sent a text, and the answer was immediate.

Supt Kent: No email sent. Leave it with me. There must be opening times for the public. Phones must be answered, or messages taken.

He showed it to the other two.

"Oh," Jellicoe said, in a small voice.

"Start by answering the phone," Charlie said, "and we'll work on some times for public access later."

She nodded. "I'd better go then, sir," she said, and Charlie realised that he had been hearing the noise of a constantly ringing phone somewhere in the building since they'd sat down.

"Hang on," he said. "DC Edwards and I need computer access and keys to the building. I want the place locked up when there's only one person here." He wanted the locks changed too. With a sinking feeling he knew that meant he would have to be the only key holder, because someone was still playing games and he didn't know who. Jellicoe stood up, and he could see new colour in her cheeks.

"I'll give you a guided tour. It'll be quick." She smiled and Charlie was pleased to see it.

The tour didn't take long, though it was accompanied by the sound of the constantly ringing telephone. It stopped, and a heartbeat later, started again. Upstairs was one big room with a single office for the senior officer, who Charlie supposed was him. Downstairs consisted of the room they had been in, a dingy interview room, plus the reception for the public and male and female locker rooms with toilets and washbasins. There was evidence of the officers who had resigned and been suspended, in the shape of untidy desks and grubby computer keyboards. Equipment for officers on patrol was hung from pegs in one corner of the big upstairs office, with radios charging on the floor underneath. It was dark and long overdue for new furniture and redecoration.

"This place is like a reverse-Tardis," Edwards said. "It doesn't look big from the outside, but it looked bigger than this."

"There are two cells," Jellicoe said. "Accessed from outside. Upstairs from them is what used to be a police flat, for a single person. But there was a leak from the roof, and it's not been used for years."

"It's awful," Charlie replied. "No one should have to work in a place like this."

"We could paint the whole place in a weekend," Edwards suggested. "Team building exercise. Or you could get on to Superintendent Kent, seeing as how you seem to have him on speed-dial. Cover up the past and make a new start."

"Please don't use the words *cover up*," Charlie said, and the anxiety lifted a little more as they all smiled at each other. Tentative smiles, but it would have to do.

"I should answer the phone," Jellicoe stood up to leave. Charlie had almost stopped hearing it.

"Record everything," Charlie said, and she nodded.

"Always, Sarge." She went to a key cabinet on the wall and produced two sets of keys. "The ones with the blue tags are the front, red for the back and green for the cells and the flat I told you about. The car keys are in the cabinet if you need them. One of the cars is in for servicing."

They all swapped numbers, and Charlie reminded Jellicoe to follow them downstairs and lock herself in when they left. "We're going to the Art College to find out about these allegedly missing students," he said.

They were heading to the door when they heard the unmistakable sound of vehicles colliding. Two car alarms went off simultaneously. Then another crash and the sound of running feet. The three of them were down the stairs and out of the door in seconds, but they were too late.

A rusty white van had ploughed into the police car at some speed, leaving them fused together like two pieces of Play Doh. Screeches and creaks filled the air as they settled. The van had ricocheted off the front of Charlie's car, but that wasn't the worst of it. The driver's side window had been smashed and the inside of his car was yellow with flames. Everything reeked of petrol.

Jellicoe spun round back into the station and returned seconds later with a fire extinguisher and was spraying Charlie's car a moment after that. It was a large cylinder, but although it seemed to dampen the fire, showed no signs of being likely to put it out. Tendrils of fire spread over the weedy tarmac towards them.

DC Edwards spoke rapidly into his phone, on to the fire brigade.

Charlie ran over to Jellicoe. "Leave it!" He grasped her arm and pulled her back towards the station when she protested. "Round the front!" He wanted the building between them and the burning car. He pushed Eddy in the same direction.

They heard the scream of the siren, and a fire engine roared into the yard.

"Fire station in the next street," Eddy shouted over the noise.

A few moments later, one of the firefighters spotted Jellicoe in her uniform and trotted towards them.

"Only take a minute," he said. "What happened?"

Charlie showed his warrant card. "We were inside when we heard the crash and the car alarms. When we came out, my car was on fire, and the window was smashed. It all stank of petrol."

The firefighter nodded. "That sounds right. Smash the window, chuck a Molotov cocktail through, and leg it. Stay here." He disappeared back round to the yard. When he came back a few minutes later, it was to tell them that the fire was out, "But you won't be driving either of those cars again, sorry."

"What about the things in my car?" Charlie asked.

The firefighter's face dropped. "I hope you're well insured, mate, because there isn't much left. And don't go messing with it. It's hot. We'll be hanging around for a while, just to make sure. We need to check for the remains of whatever they used to get it going, and you'll want to find the owners of that van."

"Which will turn out to be stolen," Edwards said. "Do you want me to check, Sarge?"

Charlie sighed. Of course, the van would turn out to be stolen, but they had to check. There might be some kind of clue about who stole it, or the owner might be the kind of person who loaned his van out to his dodgy mates. In the meantime, he had only the clothes he stood up in, and they were ripped and muddy. He was supposed to be the one in charge, and so far this morning he'd had his tires let down, been assaulted by a dog, locked out of his own police station and lost everything he owned. And it was still only just after ten in the morning. Charlie had the urge to laugh, because surely things couldn't get any worse. Except even having the thought seemed like tempting fate. Most importantly, he had no idea *why*. The tyres were, by all accounts, kids. The dog assault was about being in the wrong place at the wrong time. But being locked out was the result of a fake email, and the fire was deliberate. What he didn't know was whether it was targeting him, DS Charlie Rees, or the Llanfair police in general.

"Let's go and brew up," he said, pulling his shoulders back. He opened the front door to the police station with his newly acquired key, and the three of them trooped back inside. The telephone was still ringing.

Jellicoe boiled the kettle and made the drinks. They took the same seats as before.

"Thanks," Charlie said. "First up, is there anything

respectable I can wear hanging round the station? Or a men's clothes shop in the town? Because that was all my clothes in the boot of my car."

Jellicoe looked distraught. "What about at home, sir?"

"Don't ask," Charlie said. "I'm homeless as well. I'm booked in with Dilys at Primrose Lodge…" he got out his wallet with the address.

"I know where it is." Jellicoe said.

Edwards laughed. "Dilys is my aunt." They looked at him. He shrugged. "I assume that's why they seconded me. I was brought up here, but I've always worked in Wrexham. I'm back at my mother's house. I'd offer you some clothes, but…"

Jellicoe jumped up. "My husband is the same size as you, near enough. I'll be right back." Charlie heard her talking on the phone on the other side of the door, then she came back in. "That's sorted. Only jeans and a jumper, but it won't have paw prints up the front. And there's plenty of jackets upstairs. Marks and Spencers will do next day delivery for tomorrow."

"Thanks," Charlie said. He didn't see himself as Man at Marks and Spencer but needs must. "Now, is there anything else I should know about? Things that go with fake emails and firebombing?"

"Yesterday there were two hoax emergency calls from women saying they were being followed. We went both times, and there was no one there."

"999 calls?"

"Yes. We've got the recordings. Different women's voices. We haven't done a voiceprint or anything, but they don't sound the same."

"Anything else?"

Jellicoe shook her head, but the way she rubbed the back of her neck and then smoothed her already perfect ponytail suggested that she wasn't certain.

"There is something." Charlie said.

"I thought, and so did one of the other girls, that we *were* being followed. After dark, when we were going home. Just this last week. Nothing you could put your finger on, a feeling that's all."

"Isn't there anyone to walk you home?" Edwards asked.

Charlie stared at the big man, who had the decency to blush.

"I'm sure what DC Edwards meant to ask was were you carrying your pepper spray and handcuffs? Which I'm sure you were."

This time it was Jellicoe who blushed. "Not off duty, Sarge." Charlie opened his mouth to speak, when Jellicoe's phone rang, and she hurried out of the room. When she returned, it was with another woman in uniform.

"This is Trainee Constable Patsy Hargreaves, Sarge." Hargreaves put a carrier bag on the table. Jellicoe looked inside and handed the bag to Charlie. "I hope they fit."

"Thank you," Charlie said. "I'm sure they'll be an improvement." His phone buzzed with a text.

SUPT KENT: *Ring me*

CHARLIE EXCUSED himself and went out into the corridor.

"Sir?" he said when Kent answered.

"I need to let you know that two of the remaining staff at Llanfair have called in sick, claiming stress, and a third has resigned."

And then there were four…

5

Bright yellow jacket
MONDAY 11AM

From: the Llanfair College of Art website (Four Weeks Previously)
Llanfair College of Art welcomes record number of international students. College Principal Sir John Singer held a special Welcome Week event for students arriving from all around the world.

"This is what makes our college such an exceptional place to study," Sir John explained. "We bring together a wide range of experience and cultures in our beautiful landscape and our friendly town."

From the report of the whole College staff meeting, Llanfair College of Art

Asked about the criticism that the international students took places away from Welsh students, Sir John replied that the college was open to all.

International student fees are more than double those of home students at almost £30,000 a year. A University and College Union spokesperson said that international fees were essential to the college finances, and there was concern amongst some academics that international students faced less competition for places than did students from the UK.

. . .

CHARLIE EXPLAINED the morning's events. Kent went quiet for a moment and then said, "Work nine till five, Monday to Friday, keep the doors open but never leave anyone on their own. I'll try and get you some more help. Edwards is sound, you can trust him. Get round to that college about those missing students."

"Yes, sir."

"And watch your back. It looks civilised, but right now it's the Wild West and you're John Wayne."

"I'm thinking that I'm more of a Clint Eastwood, sir."

"I hope you're feeling lucky then. Now, I think we've pushed that metaphor as far as it's going."

Kent ended the call.

Charlie took himself off to the men's locker room. The clothes were too big and in sad colours, but they were clean, and not torn. The image in the mirror was of a man sliding ungracefully into middle age, which he absolutely wasn't, in jeans cut to conceal rather than display, and a sweater chosen for washability rather than style. His suit may have been ripped and muddy, but it was *him*. He would love to save it, if he could.

His phone rang. It was his mother. There was no point in not answering. She would simply keep ringing.

As if I wasn't feeling bad enough.

"Hi, Mum."

"Charles. We're planning a trip to Wrexham for the Cash and Carry, so we thought we'd come and see you in Melin."

He was going to have to tell her that he wasn't there anymore, ideally in a way that didn't bring his parents to Llanfair. Not while he was homeless.

"I've been seconded, Mum, and to be honest, I'm up to my eyes in it. Now isn't a good time."

"What does that mean, seconded?"

"I'll be based in Llanfair for a while. I'm in charge of looking for some missing people."

Of course, the word Llanfair would cause trouble.

"Llanfair? Where those assaults were? I hope you're not part of that, Charles. Haven't you done enough damage to this family already?"

Part of what? Assaulting women students or covering it up? Because the one thing his mother *wouldn't* think was that he'd been sent to help clear up the mess.

"The only thing I'm part of is the police. I go where I'm sent and do my job."

"And you know how I feel about it, Charles."

He tuned her out, feeling the familiar weight in his chest. If he looked in the mirror, he knew he would see his shoulders sagging. She would love the clothes he was wearing—she had been buying him garments like this for years. And if she could only persuade him to leave the police and go back to Holyhead to help run the family business, then... nope, she still wouldn't be happy.

"Sorry, Mum, I have to go."

He pressed the end call button. She would be angry, and he would pay, but for now he needed to get back to the others.

"THE VAN WAS STOLEN last night, Sarge," Edwards said to Charlie as he walked into the big office upstairs. "Nice threads." Charlie flicked a glance to where Jellicoe was on the phone, hoping Edwards got the message. A flush of pink to his cheeks showed that he had.

Charlie waited until Jellicoe had finished the call and said, "Listen up. I've spoken to Superintendent Kent, and he wants the police station open nine to five on weekdays, but no one should be here on their own. For now, there's just us four. Your colleagues have either called in sick or resigned." The two women's faces registered shock, and Hargreaves looked angry. "That isn't fair to the rest of us."

"You're right. But none of this is fair. Especially when it's people you've worked with. So, phone answering downstairs and the door open to visitors. Always think of your safety. If you need a break, lock up and stick a notice on the door saying when you'll be back. OK?" The others nodded. "DC Edwards and I are going over to the college about these missing students." He went to the rack of equipment and found a bright yellow jacket of the kind worn by uniformed officers. From the raised eyebrows, the jacket belonged to one of the women officers, but it fitted, and it would be warm. He pointedly put a pepper spray and a set of cuffs in the appropriate pockets, but decided a baton was a step too far. Then he changed his mind, and picked up a baton, too.

The disconnect between the police work he'd been doing as part of Melin Tywyll CID — a team who had worked together for years — and everything that had happened this morning was messing with Charlie's head. He was managing to put one metaphorical foot in front of the other, but none of it seemed real. He was in a police station. It might have had small windows, but the carpet was the familiar blue, the computer monitors had the Clwyd Police logo, and even the racks of hi-vis jackets and charging radios should have grounded him. Instead, his head was full of air, where thoughts, procedures and routines should have been. Automatic pilot was switched off. This stuff didn't happen. A police station in rural Wales had been attacked, police officers felt threatened, and he was homeless and without even the few possessions he'd packed into his car. He had been cut adrift from everything he knew and been told to lead the way. Somehow, wearing another man's clothes made it all harder to bear.

"Let's go, DC Edwards," he said to Edwards.

Edwards rolled his eyes.

"Eddy, please, Sarge."

"Let's go, Eddy." Because what other nickname would the guy have?

. . .

FOR ALL THAT Charlie had given Eddy the side eye about Jellicoe's ability to take care of herself, when it came down to it, he was concerned about leaving the two women on their own in the police station. Not because they were women, but because they were the last of their team, and must be feeling vulnerable. Someone had felt confident enough to attack a police station in broad daylight. The same someone might view two women as easy targets. He drew in a breath, and it was a shaky one. Eddy heard it.

"Do you want me to stay, Sarge? I don't like leaving them."

"Me neither, so we'll be quick."

"What's going on, Sarge? I mean, really, what's going on?"

The temptation was to pour out his fears to this big, confident man, and he had to hold himself back. Kent said Eddy was 'sound', but Kent wasn't here. Eddy was a local, and until Charlie had a better handle on whatever had been happening in this town, he was trusting no one. So, he focussed on the place itself.

"Tell me about the Art College," he said.

"One of the oldest centres of learning in Wales," Eddy began, sounding like a publicity website. Then he grinned. "I grew up here, and it's just part of the town. Some people resent it, see the students swanning about thinking they own the place, not speaking the language. But it's keeping the shops open, and the pubs. And they make an effort, you know? Hold events open to everyone. Encourage the students to join things in the town."

"There are people who will moan about anything," Charlie said, and without conscious thought, said it in Welsh. Eddy didn't bat an eyelid

Eddy led Charlie to the main street, as far as a mini roundabout and a war memorial tucked in next to a bank. A second street led off the roundabout at right angles. The pavements weren't crowded, but Eddy was right that the shops and cafes appeared to be thriving. There were all the essentials: chemist, optician, hardware store, more than one bank, vet's surgery, plus clothes shops (for women only, Charlie noted), charity shops and a large whole food emporium. Eddy pointed out the library and supermarket through an archway next to a shop selling Welsh blankets. On the opposite side was a high wall, lined with parked cars, and a couple of drivers blocking the road as they waited for a space.

"Free parking, see," said Eddy.

The college was behind the wall. The access was via a pedestrian gate which led to a grassy park, now scattered with fallen leaves. They followed the path to the bottom of a set of well-worn stone steps. At the top, dark wooden double doors stood open under a high archway. Once through the doors, Charlie saw that the building was only a couple of rooms deep, with another set of doors opening opposite, so that they could walk straight through to the other side.

"It's like a square donut shape," Eddy said, as they went through the second set of doors and emerged into a big space, surrounded by three stories of attractive building. The walls were a soft buttery coloured stone, and all the windows had leaded panes.

The court was lawned, with a fountain in the middle. Not a huge fountain, but a fountain, and working. Water landed almost silently in a mossy bowl, then trickled into a pool below. It must have been lovely in summer, and Charlie had a moment's regret that he had joined the police straight from school. If universities were all like this... It seemed to Charlie that this was an American Ivy League or Oxbridge college, except it was in the middle of a small Welsh town. Outside its walls there were shops selling buckets and coal scuttles, dog food and Welsh cakes. Cars blocked the road to grab a free space, or chat to their friend on the pavement. It was the kind of town where Charlie felt at home. The college was alien, but at the same time, it had been here for so long that it fitted.

"Nice, isn't it?" Eddy asked, and Charlie nodded. "We need to be on the other side," Eddy said and set off around the courtyard towards another arched doorway.

A group of students had easels set up on the grass and appeared to be drawing a pile of leaves—a Sisyphean task, as the gentlest breeze stirred the pile. Another group of students were being exhorted to *look at it, really look*. The *it* in question was the stone wall of the college. Charlie was interested, despite his lack of knowledge of anything even vaguely 'arty'.

"I never did art," Eddy said. "It clashed with rugby, but it doesn't look like I missed much."

"Fewer trips to hospital," Charlie countered, and Eddy laughed.

They climbed the steps to the door and followed the sign with a finger painted in gold indicating *College Principal* in cursive script. The sign led them up a set of polished wooden stairs to a door saying *Principal. Please knock and enter.*

Eddy knocked and they entered. The door opened onto a spacious office, with big windows looking out onto the fountain. A middle-aged woman looked up from her computer and asked how she could help.

"DC Edwards and DS Rees," Charlie said. "We're here to see the principal about some missing students?"

The woman smiled. "I'm his secretary. I'll let Dr Pennant know you're here." She picked up a phone on her desk

"I have two police officers to see you, Dr Pennant," she said. She put the phone down, stood up and walked round her desk to open a door to the neighbouring office. "Just go in. Can I bring you a coffee, or a cup of tea?" Charlie shook his head, and they followed her in. Standing behind the desk with a smile of welcome on his face, was the man who had tried to pick Charlie up the night before.

6

Scrubs up well
MONDAY 11.15AM

Messages sent three weeks previously.

Message to all LCA students from Sir John Singer, Principal

You may have heard the rumours of a series of assaults on female students. These are alleged to have taken place both on and off the campus. Please be assured that your college takes these allegations very seriously. We are working closely with Llanfair Police to establish what, if anything, has happened.

The safety of our student body is of paramount importance. If you have any information about these alleged events, please speak to one of your tutors. Women students are also advised to carry an alarm (available from the LCA shop).

Message to all LCA students from LCA Student Union

We believe women students! The attacks are real! Watch out for each other at all times—don't leave your fellow students on their own, especially after dark. Get a rape alarm (free from the union office) and carry it at all times. Your Student Union is collecting information. We are demanding college management takes this issue seriously. Find out more by attending the general meeting on Thursday at noon.

· · ·

CHARLIE STARED, his mind in turmoil. It was definitely the same man—beard, brown eyes, as tall and broad as Eddy, but without the evidence of years of rugby. Only he wasn't dressed as a lumberjack. Today, Tom was wearing a grey Prince of Wales check suit of impeccable cut, with a navy waistcoat and a pink shirt. No tattoos were visible. Charlie wondered which was the real Tom Pennant, and whether, if he had first met be-suited Tom, his reaction to the bearded man would have been different. He was acutely conscious of his own lack of sartorial elegance. Tom was staring back at him and, Charlie feared, remembering his rudeness.

It took Eddy shuffling his feet to break the silence. Charlie realised that he was expected to take the lead. To be the professional.

"Thank you for seeing us, Dr Pennant," he said. Tom shook his head as if bringing his attention back into the room.

"Please, gentlemen, have a seat. Have we offered you tea or coffee?" he asked.

"We're fine thanks, Dr Pennant," Charlie said.

"Tom, please. How can I help you today? You should understand that I'm only the acting principal. Sir John Singer has taken a leave of absence. I was abroad when the assaults took place, so if it's anything to do with that …"

That it wasn't Tom's office was clear when Charlie looked properly. Several trays of papers sat on the windowsill, as if they had been moved to make space on the desk. A paint-stained wooden box sat on the floor in the middle of the room. The walls were adorned—there could be no other word —with decidedly camp renderings of cherubs, angels and a variety of drooping figures of uncertain gender, all in ornate gold frames. He couldn't have explained it, but Charlie knew Tom hadn't chosen them. Tom saw him look.

"Hideous, aren't they? Beautifully executed sugary confections. They make my teeth ache. Sorry. You aren't here to critique Sir John's taste in art."

"We're here about two missing students," Charlie said. "Kaylan Sully and Rico Pepperdine. Rico's father has been in contact with us. What can you tell us about them?"

"Honestly? Not much."

Charlie had a copper's distrust of anyone beginning a sentence with the word "honestly". From the slight stirring in the next chair, so did Eddy.

"I have their records, such as they are, or my secretary can get them for you." Tom gave a quick smile. "I've never had a secretary before, but she seems to know everything." He stood up and went to the door, opened it and politely asked for the records.

"I never met either of them," Tom said when he came back. "Like I said, I've been away. I'm not convinced they are actually *missing*. I mean, by all accounts they're not here, but I'm not sure that constitutes *missing*."

The obvious next question was what did constitute missing, and Charlie asked it. "Not turning up to lectures, not answering their phones, absent from their accommodation, or what? Mr Pepperdine reports no phone calls, no social media presence, no contact at all for over a week. That seems like *missing* to me."

Tom cleared his throat, and made to get up, "I'll just see if Ann has got those records for you,"

"Tom, please," said Charlie, "who should we talk to about when the students were last seen or where they might be? What arrangements does the college have to monitor that students are safe and well? I'm assuming there are some procedures?"

"Procedures?" Tom asked. "Yes, of course there are procedures. They are adults, of course... but the college has a duty of care. So, we *do* ask students to leave a message with their hall warden if they are going to be off campus overnight. In case there's a fire. No one questions their right to go where they like … though we talk to them if they start missing a lot of classes."

"They didn't leave a note?"

Tom looked down at the desk. "No note."

"And when did anyone notice they weren't around?"

Tom's face flushed. "Please understand that the new students have only been here for a couple of weeks. By Christmas all the tutors will have a good idea of all the students' names. Their personal tutors will know everyone much better than that. But this early in the term… our best estimate is that they were here until the middle of last week, and they haven't been seen since. I hate to keep saying it, because it sounds like an excuse, but I've only been back for a few days. I'm a printmaker, not an administrator." He rubbed his hands over his face. "Look, I have asked around. Lots of students disappear in the first few weeks. Some go home. Some are holed up in their rooms with fresher's flu, or hangovers. They haven't found their friendship group yet. We take registers, but often they aren't up to date because people drop out or start late. If a student doesn't want to engage, that's their choice." Tom's voice had risen as he spoke. He took a breath and cupped his flaming cheeks in his hands. "And as for parents … don't forget some of these kids come to get away from their parents. We're not allowed to give information out, even to parents, without the student's written consent."

"So, essentially the college has done nothing?" Charlie asked.

Tom sighed. "Yesterday morning, their tutor group was due to go into Swansea to visit a gallery. The coach was due to leave at eight, but there was no sign of Kaylan or Rico. The tutor in charge asked the campus services officers to check their rooms, and they weren't there. They asked in the neighbouring rooms, and no one had seen either of them."

"So, you do think they're missing, as in the police should be looking for them?

"I simply don't know."

After all he had heard, nor did Charlie. But he needed to find out.

"We'd like to go and look at their rooms, now, please," he said.

TOM ASKED his secretary to call a Campus Services Officer with a full set of keys to meet them at the hall of residence entrance. Tom led them down the stairs and around the inside of the building. Several doors were standing open, showing students working in cubicles made from cheap, white-painted board. Some had easels as well. Most were covered in post-cards, sketches, pages torn from magazines and general detritus. There was surprisingly little noise, just a few soft voices. There was an overwhelming chemical smell of what Charlie supposed was paint.

The next door led them to the foyer of a library. Charlie could see the shelves of books, computer stations and yet more cubicles. Next to the check-out desk was a chocolate vending machine and a water cooler, and then they were out of the sliding glass doors and back into the sunshine. A hundred yards away was another set of glass doors to another building in front of which stood a man in navy blue trousers and a matching fleece with the college logo. The sign over the door read St Mary Hall.

"We need to see Kaylan Sully's room, and Rico Pepperdine's," Tom said, and the man led them up to two neighbouring rooms on the first floor, looking back out towards the library. Kaylan's was closest.

Kaylan's room reminded Charlie of the cells in a modern police station. Not the furnishings, but the size, the slot-shaped window and even the colour scheme of inoffensive pale blue. He wondered at the architect who could condemn hundreds of young people to minute windows in already tiny rooms. Unlike in a police station, the ambient noise was pop music rather than shouting, but the doors closed with the same heavy thump. A bench desk ran from side to side underneath the window, with a chair upholstered in pale blue, matching the easy chair on the other side of the narrow single bed. The bed had been stripped, and a clean set of bedlinen was folded on top. The room couldn't be personalised, at least not by moving the furniture — there was literally nowhere else for it to go. Charlie spied the open door of the en-suite bathroom. The cube it borrowed from the rest of the space was barely big enough for a toilet and basin, let alone a shower.

The room was overcrowded with the four of them.

"There's five of these rooms to a flat," Tom said. "Each flat has a kitchen, and there's communal space on each floor."

"It's minute," Eddy said, and Charlie silently agreed. Maybe there were downsides to university life. He couldn't imagine wanting to spend long in the tiny dark space.

Kaylan's desk was piled high with sketch books, and boxes of what looked like crayons. An unrolled paintbrush roll lay to one side, and there were two blank canvases, each about three feet square leaning against the wall next to the window. The desk wasn't tidy, but Charlie could separate the individual items, one from another. The easy chair was piled high with a mishmash of clothes, shoes, books, empty crisp packets and mobile charging cables. The smell of cleaning products competed with the odour of sweat and cheese powder.

"How would we know if anything was missing?" Eddy asked and all Charlie could do was shrug.

"Cleaners come on Thursday for this block. Students are supposed to strip their beds and tidy up, but the cleaners do their best whatever state the room is in. The fresh duvet cover and so on would have been left last Thursday" the Campus Services Officer said. "So he hasn't been back since then."

"He could have been sleeping in another student's room," Charlie said. "I think we may need to talk to the cleaners."

"I'm sure we can arrange it," Tom answered.

They trooped out of Kaylan's room and into Rico's, which by contrast was tidy as well as clean. The cleaners had presumably been able to vacuum and dust. It also had a set of bedlinen on top of a carefully folded duvet. The desk was neat, with a pile of sketchbooks next to a laptop. Paintbrushes, paints and pens were stored in a set of see-through plastic drawers, also on the desk. Rico had evidently used the drawers as his personal noticeboard. Clipped to the front was a copy of his timetable, a credit card and a couple of pieces of printed paper. Charlie looked closely. They were tickets to a gig at the Student Union, and a voucher for a curry night — both dated in the next two weeks.

Eddy was looking in the cupboards and bathroom. "He didn't take his toothbrush, Sarge, or anything else, by the looks of it. Wash bag is still here, and his duffle. These guys are definitely missing."

"We need these rooms left untouched," Charlie said. "No cleaning, no one to enter except the police."

"Unless they come back," Tom said, but he didn't sound hopeful. He led them back to his office in silence.

TOM'S SECRETARY produced the student records for Rico and Kaylan.

There were photographs as well as home addresses (in Los Angeles and Chicago respectively) and next-of-kin. Rico was dark haired with light brown skin and brown eyes. Kaylan was a yellow blond with lots of long curls pushed behind his ears.

"Around half our intake are international students," Tom

said, looking at the photographs. "Many Americans come to study here. These won't be the only two."

"How do they know to come?" Charlie asked. "I mean, who in Los Angeles or Chicago has ever heard of Wales, let alone Llanfair?"

Tom looked at Charlie with astonishment, eyes widening. "This place has an international reputation. Just because you've never heard of it …"

"Well, they'll have heard of it now," Eddy said. "If not for good reasons."

The colour drained from Tom's face.

"Yep," Eddy carried on. "And if you start losing students … and the parents start making a fuss in the media …"

Maybe I'm not the only one holding a poisoned chalice here.

Tom held his hands out, fingers splayed in a gesture of surrender. "Point taken. Let's find them. What can I do to help?"

"We need to know everyone they were in contact with," Charlie said. "Their friends, the people in their residence, the other students in their study groups, their tutors. We'll look at buses, taxis, hire cars and so on—ways they might have left Llanfair."

"Can we keep it out of the press? Please? Because this will finish us off. Seriously," Tom said. If anything, his face was even paler.

The door to Tom's office burst open, and a man in a grubby boiler suit walked in. It was the man who had been telling the students to *look, really look*, at the college wall. His brown hair stuck out from his head in big curls, and he had a brown curly beard to match. He wasn't a big man, but then bull terriers are not big dogs. This was a bull terrier of a man, and he was on the warpath. Tom's secretary was right behind him, apologies pouring from her lips. "I did tell him you were busy," she said.

The man flung his arm out, cutting the woman off,

preventing her entry to the room. "I came precisely because you were busy, Tom. Busy covering up another piece of damage wrought by the elite of the art world…"

"That would be the elite institution paying your wages, Vitruvious?" Tom stepped up to face the man, who thrust his chest out in response.

"Like you'd understand, most esteemed Principal." He bowed and then flung his arm out again, closely missing hitting the secretary in the face. "Big surprise that they chose you, with your wallpaper for the wealthy and your fellowships to New York." There was a tiny pause. Charlie watched with interest as the man took a deep breath and began to declaim like an amateur Shakespearean actor. "Rich students come here with the red carpet rolled out, while the poor die on small boats in the English Channel! That's the system your sort is upholding."

"Oh, for fucksake, V, get off your high horse before you fall off. You're hardly living on your uppers, with a place at Maes y Coed and driving a Jag. They appointed me because I was away while it was all going on. You know it as well as I do. You think I want this?"

"Power corrupts, Tom, power corrupts."

"V, these are police officers. We are discussing your missing painting students. Perhaps you'd like to give a statement?"

The man bowed to Charlie and Eddy. "Of course. Always willing to waste my time talking to the agents of the state. Though I'm a little busy with my tutorial group. Tom here will tell you how to reach me."

"Back to staring at the wall, is it, sir?" Eddy said, "Fascinating stuff."

Charlie kicked him, hoping no one was looking.

"Don't mock what you don't understand, Mr Policeman."

With another wild arm gesture, he turned and strode off.

This time the secretary stepped backwards so fast that she almost tripped.

"I tried, Tom, really I did," she said.

"Nothing any of us can do," Tom said. "Don't worry about it. Just be grateful the pretentious twat didn't persuade the Governors to appoint him Acting Principal."

The secretary visibly shuddered.

"That, gentlemen, was Inigo Vitruvious, Senior Painting Tutor, and the self-proclaimed social conscience of the college." Tom rubbed his hands over his face. "You probably should talk to him, though. Kaylan and Rico were both painting students."

Charlie felt some sympathy, if only some. Two students were missing, by any definition of the term, and the college management appeared to have done nothing except debate the term *missing* and come up with excuses. The Vitruvious man had been revolting, but it didn't mean he was wrong.

Maybe the two students had simply gone off to explore, or have a ball in Cardiff or London, but the fact remained that no one appeared to care. The college had colluded in the cover up of the assaults on female students, and their first response was to cover this up, too. He looked around him. The office was as big as the flat Charlie had left in Melin. There was room for a ten-seat conference-type table in a warm-coloured wood, highly polished, with individual blotters at each place. The chairs were upholstered in a light olive-green leather, which exactly matched the carpet and Tom's own chair. There was a wall of bookcases in the same wood as the table full of large and heavy-looking hardbacks. An enormous window dominated the side of the room between the desk and the bookcase on the opposite wall. The view was straight onto the court with the fountain, students and staff wandering along the paths or drawing leaves. Beyond was the other side of the square, a mirror image of where they sat, and beyond that, the tops of a few shops and houses and then the wooded hills that surrounded the town. At this time of year, the Welsh woodlands were spectacular. The colours against the sky looked like a postcard. Charlie coveted that view, and the lovely room, and he understood that it would be hard to give up. Except that to keep it, the college management had let their students suffer. By the sounds of it, the staff weren't suffering either. He didn't know where Maes y Coed was, but if it went with driving a Jag, it probably wasn't cheap.

7

Do you know that bloke?
MONDAY 12.30PM

From Breaking News

Still no arrests in the Llanfair assault scandal. A Clwyd Police spokesperson said that they had no comment to make, but that the alleged assaults were being taken seriously. They refused to confirm whether officers have been suspended.

A visibly distraught Jess Carter from the Llanfair College of Art Students' Union told our reporter that she had received six reports of sexual assaults on women students over the past few months.

"Obviously it's been quiet over the summer holidays, but two women were attacked in the first week of term, both new students. They've both left the college and returned home, with their education in ruins. What we don't know is whether any other women were attacked in Llanfair over the summer, or if these attacks are only on students."

Llanfair College of Art did not respond to our request for an interview.

"Do you know that bloke? The acting principal?" Eddy asked Charlie, as they walked back through the courtyard. Students were still drawing piles of leaves, but the group staring at the wall had gone, along with their tutor.

"We've met," Charlie said, as repressively as he could.

"Because he surely recognised you. And was looking at you like I'd look at a triple chocolate cookie."

Charlie laughed. "Not a good image, Eddy, mate."

"True though. Triple chocolate cookies are excellent. It's a compliment. We can pick some up on our way back and you'll see. You're a bit of a triple chocolate cookie yourself."

"Could we think about work instead?"

"Sure. But you are gay, right?"

"Yes!" Charlie almost yelled. "Work, DC Edwards. Concentrate on work. I want to send Jellicoe and Hargreaves out to ask some questions—together, mind. Perhaps the delightful Vitruvious will be better behaved talking to women. They can canvas the other students while they're there. I want you to talk to the owner of that white van from this morning and do a house to house round the police station in case anyone saw anything."

"Will do. And you, Sarge? Reporting back to the Super? That man's a legend. A legend, I tell you."

"He's a good boss."

"He's got the best clear-up rate in Clwyd. And he's a bit of a triple chocolate cookie, if you know what I mean."

Charlie could hardly pretend Superintendent Mal Kent wasn't seriously good-looking. Equally, discussing the man's appearance wasn't the professional detective he wanted to portray.

"Let's get back. I need to think."

And buy myself some new clothes. Because I can't wear these for much longer.

WAS it wrong to spend work time buying new clothes? Charlie decided it wasn't, given how he had lost every garment he possessed in the service of his job. He allowed himself half an hour online bought the essentials gave the police station as the delivery address, pressed Pay and gave them his bank card details. *Not* the way he wanted to spend his working day. Patsy Hargreaves and Mags Jellicoe had gone to start enquiring about the missing students, Eddy was on the phone to the owner of the white van, and the front door to the police station was once again, locked. Time to unlock it. He could think while he answered the phone.

Perhaps he shouldn't have been surprised that the first call he answered was from Tom Pennant. He had left a card with his mobile number after all.

"Tom," he said. "What can I do for you?"

There was a silence from the other end.

"Tom?"

"Sorry. I probably need to apologise, if I came on a bit strong last night. And I wanted to know how you were?" Tom added.

"No need for apologies, and I'll be fine."

"Could I take you for dinner? Because I think I do need to apologise."

Would you wear the suit? Or come with the tats on show and the lumberjack outfit? Not sure which I'd prefer. But FFS would you think about how it might look?

"Tom. Think about it. The police and the college management are—possibly—recovering from a major collusion and cover-up scandal. Let's not start another one, hey?"

"But that was nothing to do with either of us!"

"You think the media would notice that? Do you think your Vitruvious guy wouldn't make a point of calling them?"

"Maybe you're right, but I would like to get to know you better."

Charlie thought that dinner with Tom might be a nice way to spend an evening, but what he wanted and what he could have were two very different things. The image of his grandma telling his mother that *Charlie never asks for sweets when we're out* came into his mind. He never asked, because his mother didn't like children who 'demanded.' She didn't approve of sweets either, come to that. She would probably approve of Tom, or at least approve of his status as the principal of an important institution. If she did, she would assume... oh to hell with his mother.

"Sorry, Tom, but it's really not a good idea."

"Perhaps when this is all over then."

This is never going to be over. But he didn't say that. And he didn't know whether he was thinking about the state of policing in Llanfair, or his bloody mother's disapproving voice in his head.

When Charlie's phone rang again, he almost didn't answer. He had failed to expel his mother's disapproval from his mind, so he assumed it was her. There had been demoralisation enough for one day. But before he could cut her off, he saw that it was an unknown number. Probably a fake parcel delivery, but he answered anyway.

"DS Rees? This is Nigel Harrington-Bowen. *Inspector* Harrington-Bowen. We need to talk. When can you be available?"

That would be Inspector Nigel Harrington-Bowen, suspended for being up to his eyes in the cover up of the assaults on young women.

"I think you need to talk to Superintendent Kent about that, sir."

"Don't be ridiculous, Rees. You need to understand what's going on in Llanfair, and who has been doing the proper police work in this town. Kent has no idea. In fact, Kent and his *friends* may not be around to cause trouble for much longer."

"Is that so, sir?" Charlie said, as woodenly as he could. "I'll be pleased to talk to you." Which was a complete lie. "Perhaps I could call you back?" Charlie had no intention of ever calling back.

· · ·

THE OFFICE where Charlie was now sitting had the name 'Inspector Harrington-Bowen' on the door. The room was even smaller and more cluttered than the space outside. The top of the desk was covered in paper, mostly brown cardboard files, scribbled-on writing pads and indecipherable post-it notes. To use the computer keyboard, Charlie had moved drifts of paper, and had to dust the monitor with a piece of kitchen roll. The room had another one of the tiny windows, admitting next to no light. To be able to see, the overhead fluorescent tube was on, despite the faint buzz it made. The only good thing about the office was the comfortable fabric covered seat, some kind of hybrid between an armchair and a desk chair. This space didn't suggest *proper police work* to Charlie.

Charlie had no doubts about what was meant by Superintendent Kent's *friends*. He was one of them. Kent's reputation was of support for minorities — which included women, a minority in the police. He'd also gone out on a limb, more than once, to root out corruption. So he wasn't popular with the old guard, but Harrington-Bowen had sounded as if he knew something, something more than the usual schoolboy name-calling. Charlie added it to his mental list of *things I need to find out -- though not by talking to Harrington-Bowen*

Charlie made a pile of the cardboard files, sneezing as dust filled the air. He started to go through them one at a time, intending to sort them into those needing action, and those that could be left. Half an hour, and many sneezes later, he had two files he considered important. Both were marked No Case. They were both complaints about sexual misconduct by Harrington-Bowen's sergeant, Jared Brody. The rest were interesting, in that they threw light onto what Harrington-Bowen thought was important. He opened the desk drawers in search of a pen and paper. He found them. He also found a data stick with a playboy bunny logo, a half bottle of whiskey, a multipack of rolls of mints, a toiletries bag with shaving kit, toothbrush and cologne (Lynx. Lynx for a grown man…) a comb and a packet of condoms. In another drawer was a badly folded shirt in a plastic carrier bag, When Charlie lifted it out, a pair of well-washed navy-blue poly cotton boxer shorts fell onto the floor. He had a bad feeling about the data stick, and it didn't take much in the way of his detective skills to work out that Harrington-Bowen used his office to get ready for assignations. With some trepidation, Charlie pushed the data stick into the computer and pressed play. It was porn. Porn featuring a faceless man masturbating in front of a frightened-looking woman.

I'm going to have to watch this. In the full knowledge that it was probably planted, because who would leave it to be found in their desk drawers?

This just got worse and worse.

There was a knock at the door. Charlie clicked the screen to black, his heart beating overtime as he did so. It was ridiculous. The porn wasn't his, it was part of the investigation, but no way did he want anyone else to see it on his computer. Not that he was embarrassed to say that he watched porn, sometimes, in private, but …

"Come in," he jumped up and opened the door, telling his insides to behave. "PC Jellicoe."

"Mags, please, Sarge."

"Mags. What's up?"

"We just got back from the college and there was a call from some police station in England." Mags, said *England* in the way most British people would have said *Outer Mongolia* or *Uzbekistan*. "One of your missing students, the Kaylan guy, just walked in, and said he'd been kidnapped. He escaped, but he says his friend didn't. He thinks his friend may be dead."

"Kidnapped. Shit. OK, let's have what you've got."

She gave Charlie a post-it with a telephone number and the words *Brocklehurst, Gtr Manchester.*

"The sergeant said Kaylan was in a bit of a state. They've taken him to A and E. Just dehydrated according to the docs."

"Thanks, Mags."

Charlie's head was buzzing. If the second student was still missing, possibly injured or worse, one of them needed to talk to Kaylan. But there would be a jurisdiction problem. He picked up his phone and called Mal Kent.

"Sir, we've located one of the students…" he began to explain, but Kent interrupted.

"Listen, Charlie, I've been called into see the Chief Constable. I'm expecting to be put on gardening leave. For now, you're on your own. You'll have a couple of days before they work out where you are and what you're doing. Sorry, I have to go." There was a pause, but Charlie heard the sound of quiet voices at the other end. Then, "I will be fine. But you may not be, and if they come for you, they'll come for Edwards and Hargreaves too. Keep an eye out for Jared Brody. He was the sergeant at Llanfair, and our techies think his prints are all over that fake email from me. There are people who don't want any more light shining on Llanfair police. Get as much as you can out into the open. Two days, Charlie and the clock is ticking." Then he was gone.

The spike of panic in Charlie's chest was back, and it had brought friends. He couldn't breathe. He wanted to throw up. Fuck, he was *going* to throw up. He ran for the toilet, leaving Mags staring after him in confusion.

CHARLIE WASHED HIS FACE, and told himself to get a grip. The clothes he was forced to wear, the dreadful night, the headache, the endlessly ringing phone, the fate of the missing students, and now Kent's call. Panic was waiting to engulf him, and no amount of deep breathing or counting to ten was having any effect. If he got it wrong four people would be out of a job, but the chances of *him* getting it right seemed less than zero.

"You alright, Sarge," Mags called through the door.

"No," he answered, honestly.

He threw some more cold water on his face, and mopped it up with a handful of cardboard-like paper towels. The door opened, and Mags burst in, took one look at his face and threw her arms round him. Her body was soft, and the contact was comforting. It was enough that this time the deep breaths worked. He stepped backwards, and so did Mags.

"Thanks," he said. "Really, thanks."

The banging of doors and a call of "Hello?" announced that Eddy was back from his house-to-house.

Charlie had to make a choice, and he made it.

"Stick a notice on the front door saying we'll open again at two, and meet me in the break room," he said to Mags. "I need to tell you all what's going on."

8

Triple Chocolate Cookie
MONDAY 1PM

Exclusive: Gay Cop slept as his lover murdered sexy lifeguard in the next room! See pages 15 and 16 for the full story.

FIVE MINUTES LATER, Charlie had a coffee in front of him, and was trying to decide whether eating a triple chocolate cookie would settle his stomach or send him running back to the gents. He decided to risk it. Eddy was munching his way through his second cookie and lining up his third. Patsy Hargreaves was close behind in the cookie-eating stakes. Mags was nibbling hers, very, very slowly. Eddy raised his eyebrows at her. "Cousin's wedding coming up," she said. "I'm a matron of honour, and my dress is already too small."

"What's a matron of honour?" Eddy asked, between bites.

"God knows," Mags said.

"It is a married woman who supports the bride," Patsy said. "A largely redundant role, in the modern world, but often given to friends of the bride who are unable to be bridesmaids."

"Thank you, Wikipedia," said Eddy.

Patsy looked faintly puzzled.

"Enough," Charlie said. "I need to talk to you, and I'm trusting you to keep what I say confidential. You have to trust that I'm telling the truth."

"What happens if we aren't trustworthy?" Patsy asked.

"We all lose our jobs," Charlie said, "and the people who covered up the assaults on young women get away with it."

"And if we are trustworthy?" Patsy sat forward in her chair, chin on her hands, looking at Charlie for an answer. But it was Eddy who replied.

"Probably the same." He held his hand up to prevent another question from Patsy. "But if we don't at least try, the bad guys are bound to win."

"Do, or don't do," Patsy said with a grin. She and Eddy chorused: *"there is no try."*

Mags gave an audible sigh. "There's a notice on the door saying we'll be re-opening in an hour."

Charlie smiled. It was ridiculous, but the squabbling felt like the beginnings of teamwork, in an odd kind of way.

"Mags is right," he said. "We haven't got long. So here it is."

He told them what Mal Kent had told him, about how they were on their own, about Jared Brody, and about the phone call from Nigel Harrington-Bowen. Then he took a deep breath.

"I'm only a DS, but I'm the ranking police officer so I used Harrington-Bowen's office. The place is a mess. I sorted out the files he'd left. Most of them are about fairly minor crimes. There are two cases alleging sexual misconduct by his sergeant: Jared Brody. I also found some disturbing evidence that either Harrison-Bowen has been set up, or that he was abusing his position … and if he was, it was probably to get sexual favours."

Mags dropped her mug. It didn't break, but cold coffee splashed onto her trousers and dribbled onto the floor.

"Shit. Sorry." She produced a tissue from her pocket and began dabbing at the liquid. Her face had gone white.

"Mags?" Charlie said.

Mags carried in trying to clean up.

Eddy leaned over and picked up the mug. He reached for the roll of kitchen paper and handed it to Mags.

"I caught him," Mags said, "in his office with a woman. You know … having sex. I think he was in the middle of a divorce, and not his first. I thought he was a total creep, but some women liked him."

"Creep, IMO." Patsy said. "He tried it on with me once and I threatened to kick him in the balls. He said I'd never make it out of probation. I said I'd report him for harassment. He'd been reported before."

"How the hell do you know that?" Eddy asked.

Patsy shrugged. "He's a stupid man. Left the letter with the disciplinary hearing date in the photocopier. I took a copy for myself, then I gave him the original back. He knew I'd read it."

"Jesus," Eddy said, "remind me not to get on the wrong side of you."

"Don't be a creep, and you won't," Patsy said. "Though to be completely fair, Brody was a bigger creep. He used to send pop-up dick pics to women officers' computers."

"There was a data stick in the desk drawer" Charlie said, wresting control of the meeting back, making a mental note to come back to Jared Brody. "It has a pornographic video. I thought it must have been planted. Maybe I'm wrong. If I am, we've got some leverage. But regardless of that, we need to find out who set fire to the cars in the yard, why someone, probably Brody, sent that bogus email from Superintendent Kent, and what happened to the two students. So, reports please. Eddy?"

"White van man, aka Molotov cocktail man," Eddy said. "Two people saw him well enough to give me a description.

Young man, skinny, grey trackies, black trainers, black bomber jacket, black gloves, and a faded black baseball cap with some kind of white logo, pulled low to cover his face. Not pulled low enough to hide a pathetic ginger beard. Pathetic in that it's a pathetic amount of hair, not that it's ginger. One of the witnesses is from the hairdresser across the road, the other is an old gent from the house next door to here. Neither of them saw the van arrive, but they heard the crash and went to look. Both of them saw him run off towards the playing fields. From there he can basically disappear into the woods, or back into town."

"What's really interesting," Eddy went on, "is that the owner of the white van used it for his gardening business."

"Petrol, for all that gardening equipment," Mags interrupted,

"Petrol," Eddy confirmed. "Petrol and an apprentice. A young lad called Gwilym. I can't help wondering what Gwilym looks like."

"Find out," Charlie said. Eddy nodded. Then he looked sadly into the cookie bag, shook the last crumbs out onto his hand and licked them up.

"Gross," Mags said.

"Don't start," Charlie said. "Mags. What about Vitruvious?"

"No idea," Patsy said. "Disappeared."

"We spoke to his students," Mags said, "but he had gone, and no one knows where. We got his home address and phone, but he's not answering his phone. He lives about five miles out of town in a village called Maes y Coed, so we can't get there without a car. Mind you, they probably wouldn't let us in, even if we had a car. Millionaires row. My Gran says there isn't a house in the whole village for less than six hundred grand."

"So, not completely millionaire's row, then. Anyway, the car's in bits," Patsy added, as if it was news.

"We *know*," Eddy said. "We were there. And millionaire's row is a figure of speech."

"I was just explaining…"

"What *did* you find?" Charlie said. The effort of keeping his colleagues on track was damping down the panic. He was self-aware enough to recognise that he had been the joker in the past. The temptation was to join in, a temptation he resisted, though not without an internal smile.

"Not much," Mags said. "The students we spoke to were in the painting tutor group. They said Kaylan in particular was a big Vitruvious fan. A couple of them said Vitruvious was one of the reasons they had applied to the college, but they found the reality wasn't so exciting. *Bit of a prat* according to one student. *Goes on and on about inequality and refugees. Says our work must have a social message. Then he turns up in a posh car.* Another said she thought he was going to have favourites, and that Kaylan was a suck up, despite not being much of an artist. *Wanted to be in the in-crowd.* No idea if any of it was true. They've only been at college for a few weeks."

"Anything else?" Charlie asked.

"We went to the hall of residence and asked around. *One* young woman obviously liked Rico. Said he had a cool tattoo of a "lonesome pine" on his shoulder. A few people said he was as thick as two planks, and a brilliant painter. The consensus among the few people we saw was that Kaylan and Rico were quiet, as in not noisy, and that they had takeaways most nights—which was apparently because they were Americans," Mags said. "But they've turned up. So a lot of what we did was a waste of time."

"Only one of them," Charlie reminded her. "We need to get up there and talk to Kaylan ASAP. Rico is still missing. They've been gone for a week, and I don't think they went willingly."

He explained what he and Eddy had seen in the hall of residence. "Rico had left his credit card and his toothbrush.

He had tickets for events in the next few weeks. All the evidence was that they expected to be back pretty soon."

"Except, we can't go to Brocklehurst without a car," Patsy pointed out.

"I have a car," Eddy said.

"OK. Here's the plan," Charlie said. He wasn't sure it was the best plan, but they needed to keep moving, and there wasn't time for a thorough evaluation of all the possible options. "Eddy and I will go up to Brocklehurst and talk to Kaylan, bring him back if we can. We need to know if there's anything in this idea that Rico is dead. Either way, we need to keep looking for Rico.

"Patsy and Mags, get onto the owner of the white van and get a description of this Gwilym. If he sounds like our fire-starter, make sure you know where we can pick him up. I'm really sorry, but I need you to look at the data stick video. It's not going to be fun, not if it's all like the bit I saw. But you two worked here. What I saw looked pretty amateur, and if it was made by someone here, you're the most likely to recognise something or someone. Last of all, get onto the garage and see if we can get the other car back. If they say no, find somewhere to hire one. Back here at five if we can."

He stood up and brushed the crumbs from his trousers. The others did the same. Eddy offered them all a high five. "All for one," he said, with a big grin. Charlie rolled his eyes.

"Let's get going," he said.

EDDY LED Charlie to a big car park on the street behind the police station. He pointed to a terrace of houses on one side of the car park. "Mum's house. And Aunty Dilys's place where you'll be staying is down there." He pointed at a street on the other side, going off at right angles. Most of the houses were rendered and painted in a variety of colours, ranging from cream and white to bright blue. The overall effect was oddly harmonious. "We're going to be neighbours." He produced a set of keys from his pocket and there was a bleep as he unlocked a grey VW Golf, not much different to the one currently sitting burned-out in the police station yard, covered in foam. "Hop in. Chuck that stuff in the back."

The stuff was a pair of trainers the size of small boats, and a black hoodie Charlie could have used as a tent. Eddy had the driver's seat so far back that no one could sit behind him.

"I'll get directions," Charlie said, and got out his phone, noting approvingly that Eddy had a charging cable hanging invitingly from the dashboard. The phone told him the trip would take an hour and a half, so there was little chance of their being back for five. He said as much to Eddy.

"I think I can improve on that, Sarge," he said.

9

Playlist
MONDAY 2.30PM

From: Breaking News

Welsh flasher threatens women with 'huge knife'. The small north Wales town of Llanfair is reeling from a series of knife attacks on young women. The flasher reportedly chooses his victims and cuts their clothes with a knife before forcing them to watch him masturbate. Breaking News understands that to date, no women have been injured.

EDDY OBSERVED THE SPEED LIMITS, in that he drove as fast as they permitted. He had good reactions—he needed them at the speed he drove—and Charlie thought that the car had much better acceleration than his own version. The way Eddy pushed the car, overtook without hesitation and scraped through the occasional traffic light at the very last minute would undoubtedly shave time off the journey.

"I trained as a traffic cop," Eddy said when Charlie commented. "I've done every driving course on offer. But in the end, it wasn't for me. High speed chases are bloody dangerous."

"This car looks the same as mine—before the fire, obviously. But it seems more powerful."

Eddy grinned. "I may or may not have made a few changes. I may or may not be a bit of a speed queen."

Charlie smiled back. There was nothing he could do until they arrived, so he could relax and enjoy the ride. Eddy turned the music up, loud enough to enjoy, but not so loud as to make conversation difficult. First up was George Ezra, and both of them sang along, Eddy marking time on the steering wheel, while still managing to whip the car in and out of slower traffic.

THE FIRST FEW miles were the reverse of the journey Charlie had made earlier, along the wide river valley to the coast. After that it was the expressway, and then the tangle of motorways around the outskirts of Manchester. The mountains and forests were replaced by lines of high-side lorries heading to and from the Holyhead ferries to Ireland. Once they crossed the border into England, the satnav came into its own as motorways split and merged, with signposts pointing to places they didn't want to go.

"What's it like working with Kent?" Eddy asked, when they'd navigated their way onto a reasonably clear stretch. "I mean, he gets results, but he's not universally popular at HQ."

"Popularity isn't everything. He's a good boss." Charlie said.

"So how come he sent you here?"

This wasn't a conversation Charlie wanted to have, though at this point he didn't have much left to lose.

"He sent me here to get me out of the way. I'm sure you saw my picture in the papers. Everyone else did." Eddy looked embarrassed. Of course he'd seen.

"Let's just say, I wouldn't climb over you in bed to go and murder someone." Eddy said with a grin.

Charlie shrugged, determined to ignore the comment. "I expected to have to resign, quite honestly."

"That's the police," Eddy said. "Favours swapped around. The only difference between people like Kent, and my DCI and the Harrington-Bowens of this world, is that none of us are in the Masons."

"How do you know your DCI isn't in the Masons?"

"She's called Freya Ravensbourne. Last I heard, women are still unwelcome."

"Is that the only difference, though?" Charlie asked. "Because what I did was make a stupid mistake. What these guys did was deliberate."

Eddy overtook a procession of lorries before answering.

"I'm here because DCI Ravensbourne owes Kent a favour. That's what she told me anyway. She said he wanted someone quote *sound* unquote to work in Llanfair, and I drew the short straw. It seems to me that Kent is pulling all the strings, and we're the puppets dangling on the end."

"Sometimes we have to choose a side. I'm choosing Kent over the likes of Harrington-Bowen."

The music had segued into Taylor Swift, and Charlie and Eddy listened without speaking for a while.

"We need to think about this Kaylan character," Charlie said. He saw Eddy's hands relax infinitesimally on the wheel and heard him let out a long breath. The awkwardness could be forgotten for now.

BROCKLEHURST WAS an ex-industrial town that had somehow morphed into somewhere trendy and desirable. The houses were the same narrow stone terraces as in the neighbouring, unfashionable towns, but in Brocklehurst, they'd been gussied up with window boxes, and there were bicycles chained to the railings in front of many of the houses. The high street had been pedestrianised, and independent shops and cafes were thriving alongside the Spar, Greggs, and Bargain Booze. Charlie and Eddy found the police station easily enough, and explained to the desk sergeant why they were there. He was a well-rounded figure in a uniform that didn't fit. Charlie deduced that the man was losing weight but hadn't yet lost enough for a smaller size.

The sergeant shook hands with both of them over the reception counter. They were not invited any further in. "You coming to take the lad back to the land of our fathers? He's still in the hospital, but they don't need to keep him much longer. You can pick him up from there."

"Have you spoken to him about his friend?" Charlie asked.

"He wasn't making a lot of sense, so not really. I told your girl, he says his friend is dead, but that was about all he did say." Charlie winced at the man calling Mags their 'girl'.

"Has anyone informed his next of kin?" Charlie asked.

"I think the nurses were seeing to that," the man said. He didn't sound certain. It would be one of the things they would need to check.

"Let me get this clear," Eddy said. "Kaylan says he was kidnapped, and his friend is dead, but you haven't taken a statement? And you are quite happy for us to take over, even though Kaylan appeared on your patch?"

Charlie wanted answers to those questions, but he didn't want the locals getting all defensive. He needed to channel some of Mal Kent's charm. He put his hand on Eddy's arm, and kicked his ankle where it couldn't be seen.

"I think what my colleague means is that we don't want to step on anyone's toes. As Kaylan appeared in your area, his friend Rico could be around here too, and he might be injured, or worse."

The desk sergeant shrugged. "Could be. And if the lad starts making sense, we'll take his statement and start a search if it's called for." He pushed a card across the counter. "Give me a ring when you've seen him. But we close at five, mind."

Charlie sensed Eddy was about to speak, so he kicked him again.

"Thank you," Charlie said, and politely asked for directions to the hospital, which turned out to be back the way they had come.

As they headed to the door, The desk officer called after them. "It'll be a cold day in hell before we need Taffys from Llanfair telling us how to do our jobs. Or poofters who fuck murderers. Now piss off."

"It seems to me," Eddy said once they were outside, "that guy would fit in well with Harrison-Bowen and his gang."

"Agreed," Charlie replied.

THEY FOUND Kaylan Sully sitting on a hospital bed with his feet up, and his back against a pile of pillows. He looked like the picture in his file, but paler and grubbier. There were shadows under his eyes. His hair needed a wash, he had a week's worth of blond stubble and his clothes looked as if he had slept in them. He wore a plastic hospital bracelet, and the back of his left hand had a blob of cotton wool fastened in place with several strips of sticky fabric tape.

"Hey," he said, when the nurse introduced Charlie and Eddy. "You gonna take me home, because I think I'm wearing out my welcome here."

"Home being Llanfair? Or Chicago?"

Kaylan held a hand up, as if warding them away, and frowned.

"Not Chicago. I need to get back to college. I've missed a week. These people say I'm fine to go, just dehydrated and they've sorted that." He showed them the hand with the plaster. "I've had bags full of hydration."

"Can you tell us where you've been? And where Rico is?" Charlie asked.

Kaylan looked Charlie directly in the eyes. His stare was disconcerting, because it was so deliberate. Kaylan wanted

Charlie to see him looking. Wanted Charlie to see that he had nothing to hide. Maybe he didn't.

"I don't know where I've been, and I don't know where Rico is. I know I'm in a hospital near Manchester, and that some police from a dinky village brought me here. I can remember being in my room at the college, and the next thing, I'm outside a police station somewhere I've never heard of. And they keep telling me I've been missing for a week. I've had my mom and dad in hysterics, threatening to make me go home. I had to get one of the nurses to calm them down."

He swung his legs over the side of the bed.

"Can we go?"

Eddy stepped into Kaylan's personal space.

"This isn't a taxi service, mate. This morning you told the local coppers that Rico was dead. Now you're saying you don't remember anything. Which one is it?"

"Hey, officer, back up. I told you I don't remember, and I don't remember saying Rico was dead either."

Eddy didn't move.

"You've been gone a week, and all that's wrong with you is dehydration. Are you seriously expecting us to believe you have no idea how you got from north Wales to greater Manchester?"

"Yes. That's exactly what I expect you to believe, because that's what happened. Now I'm going back to college, and if you aren't going to take me, I'll get someone here to call me a cab."

This time Eddy did take a step backwards. "We'll take you back to Llanfair, Kaylan, but don't think for a minute that you're finished with us."

The drive back to Llanfair was as quick as the drive to Brocklehurst. Clearly Eddy had one way of driving, and it was as fast as he could. Kaylan sat in the back seat, behind Charlie, and sulked. Charlie marvelled that anyone could sulk for an hour without speaking, though he had grown up with a woman who could radiate disapproval for days. *Same thing, I suppose.* With Kaylan in the back, they couldn't discuss the case, so Eddy put his music back on. Charlie listened happily, trying to concentrate on the songs rather than the potential disasters waiting back in Llanfair. Rico was still missing, Kaylan's story made no sense, there were porn videos in the police station, someone had firebombed his car, his boss was in trouble... round and round went the thoughts. Glancing over at Eddy, Charlie suspected that similar thoughts were chasing themselves in Eddy's head.

Back in Llanfair, Eddy whipped through a couple of back streets, and ended up outside the entrance of St Mary's Hall, the student residence. The walls of the art college were visible through a stand of leafless trees. He clicked the locks on the car so Kaylan couldn't get out.

"We need to talk to you in the morning," Eddy said. "Charge up your phone and don't even think of not answering it."

Charlie turned round. "Rico is still missing, and sorry, Kaylan, but you're what we've got. I know you say you don't remember, but with a good night's sleep, something might come back."

Kaylan was evidently still sulking, but he nodded. "Sure. I'm not going anywhere," he said, then looked pointedly at the door. Eddy flipped the release button, and Kaylan got out and disappeared into the building, leaving the car door open behind him.

"Tosser," said Eddy as Charlie undid his seatbelt and levered himself out of the car to close the back door. He had stiffened up during the drive and had begun to fantasise about a hot shower and a soft bed. But they still had work to do.

"Did you believe any of that?" Eddy asked when Charlie climbed back in.

"He'd have been more convincing if he hadn't changed his story from *Rico is dead* to *I can't remember anything.* But we'll ask again in the morning. In the meantime, let's see what Mags and Patsy have been up to."

Eddy parked back on the big car park. There was a pay and display machine, but Eddy ignored it. They walked the few hundred yards back to the station. The smell of burned plastic hung in the air by the back door, and Charlie gave himself a moment to wonder if any of his possessions could be saved. A glance at the mangled ruins gave him the answer. Eddy held the door open for Charlie, taking up most of the doorway and forcing Charlie to squeeze past. Eddy moved, his massive thigh brushing Charlie's arse. Was it deliberate? Charlie couldn't tell, and he didn't have the bandwidth to worry about it, because coming from the break room was the unmistakable sound of a woman crying.

10

Define 'Assault'

MONDAY 5PM

From: Local radio drive time

DJ: We have a Jeff from Llanfair. What did you want to say Jeff?

Jeff: There are all these stories about Llanfair and I wanted to say that it's a great place to live.

DJ: Great to hear, Jeff. What about these attacks on students we keep hearing about?

Jeff: That's for the police to deal with. We need more bobbies on the beat. Sometimes the police station isn't open for days. Dunno why it's there really.

DJ: That doesn't sound good.

Jeff: There's always a copper around if you go a mile over the speed limit though.

DJ: Ain't that the truth, Jeff? Now, what about a bit of music....?

It was Mags who was crying. Patsy sat awkwardly on the other side of the low table, holding out a piece of kitchen roll. Both women looked up as Charlie and Eddy entered the room. Mags grabbed the kitchen roll from Patsy and blew her nose, mopping up the tears. Her face was left red and blotchy, with smears of mascara on her cheeks. Patsy got up for more kitchen roll and passed it over. Mags took the paper, but mumbled an apology and ran out of the room.

"Coffee," Charlie said, heading for the kettle. They would all feel better fortified with caffeine. Well, he would, anyway.

The carpet in front of the mini-kitchen was worn. It wasn't quite through to the underlay, but the woven tan fibres of the backing were starting to show. All around the worn patch were dark stains from dripping tea bags and dropped milk. In the middle of the room, the carpet was blue, though it too was patterned with stains and ground-in dirt. In the background, the phone was still ringing, clicking on to the answering machine, stopping for a moment and starting to ring again. It reminded him to call both Kaylan and Rico's parents. It was something he should have done earlier. How the hell was he supposed to keep all these plates spinning at once?

The kettle boiled and clicked off. Charlie found four clean mugs on the draining board — either Patsy or Mags had washed up. It was time to open a new jar of coffee. Charlie peeled the foil back and inhaled the scent, wishing that instant coffee tasted half as good as that smell. He felt Eddy looming behind him, very close. Was it deliberate? Patsy interrupted the moment before he could decide.

"There's sandwiches in the fridge. Mags' husband brought them. Home-made, nice. We saved you some."

At the word 'sandwiches' Charlie suddenly felt his empty belly. Neither he nor Eddy had eaten anything since the cookies at lunchtime, and even if Eddy had eaten half the bag, he must be hungry too.

"Thank God for Mr Mags," Eddy said, opening the fridge door. He took the cling-film covered plate of triangular sandwiches made from thick-sliced multi-seed bread to the table and unwrapped it. Yellow cheese and dark brown pickle showed between the slices of bread, and Charlie could almost feel his teeth cutting through the cheese, and the salty taste on his tongue.

"Don't you dare eat them all," Charlie warned.

The answer was no more than an acknowledgement, mumbled around half a sandwich. Cheese and pickle. I love cheese and pickle, Charlie thought, salivating as he picked up the sweet smell of the pickle. The truth was, he would have loved any kind of sandwich filling, up to and including fried horse. He put four cups of coffee on the table, with the bag of sugar, two clean spoons, and a carton of milk. Then he grabbed a sandwich, and managed to eat half of it before Mags came back. Her eyes were still red, but the mascara smudges had gone.

"Sorry about that," she said.

Charlie swallowed, and pushed one of the mugs of coffee towards her.

"Sit down," he said, "and let's have a catch-up. Thanks for the food."

Eddy was inhaling sandwiches as fast as he could, so Charlie grabbed himself another one before the plate was empty. It was cold from the fridge, so he warmed his hands on the mug of hot coffee.

"You two first," he said, looking at Mags and Patsy.

"We watched the videos on the data stick," Patsy said. "We did everything else on the list too, in case you were wondering, *and* answered the phone *and* took a report of a lost dog from a member of the public. In between, we watched the videos. Mags is upset because we think they're videos of the assaults on students, and we think one of them is from last week. One that neither of us think was ever reported."

"Because," Mags said, "the dinosaurs running this police station said it wasn't assault if the perpetrator didn't touch the victim. But it *is*."

"Sexual Offences Act, 2003, section 66," Patsy said. "Showing your genitals with the intention of frightening someone gets you up to two years inside. And that's what's on the video. This poor woman cowering in a corner, while a bloke whose face we can't see is having a wank. Bastard."

The sandwich turned to cotton wool in Charlie's mouth. He put the remains down on the plate, and saw Eddy do the same. Charlie took a swallow of his coffee, though it tasted of nothing. It was something to do, something that didn't involve running around, screaming, and breaking things.

"It was horrible," Mags said. "This poor woman was terrified, and then the bloke just zips himself up and walks off."

Charlie fixed on something Patsy had said.

"What makes you think this woman didn't report the assault?" he asked.

The two women looked at each other, then Mags spoke.

"Patsy saw the pattern," she said. "Patsy was the first one to realise that this wasn't some random flasher. Because the word from Harrington-Bowen was that nothing was happening. We were basically told to take the reports and pass them to him. When we asked about them, he said there was no case to answer, or that the perpetrator was imaginary, or the victim had a history of crying wolf, or had changed her story. But Patsy made copies of everything, and that's how it all came out. After a bit, I started helping. So between us, we've met most of the women and read all the reports. This woman never came forward. But Patsy thinks she knows where it happened, and that it only happened a few days ago."

"There's a poster. You can see it, and it only went up last week," Patsy said. "So, the people covering up have all gone, and there's been lots of publicity, but this guy is still attacking women."

THERE WAS no way Charlie could keep this information from Tom, in his Acting Principal role. Whether Tom would do anything to warn the student body remained to be see. They had a picture of the flasher, but it wasn't enough to make an identification, not yet.

Charlie rang Tom's number, imagining him in a luxurious flat, walls lined with bookcases and pictures. Better pictures than those on his office walls. Interesting pictures. But when Tom answered, Charlie heard the unmistakable sound of a busy pub.

"Hang on," Tom said.

Charlie heard the clicks and burps of a phone being carried through a crowd, the click of a door opening and Tom's voice. "That's better. What can I do for you? Because whatever it is, you should probably come down here for your dinner. The curry is to die for."

"I need to talk to you. As the college principal."

"Come to the pub. You can talk to me here, while we eat. The Three Horseshoes. It's only a hundred yards from the cop shop. I've even got a table. I'll order and then we won't have long to wait. Say yes."

This was the Tom who didn't take no for an answer. Though fair play, last night he'd appeared genuinely concerned about Charlie's potential hangover, and his state of mind. Was that really only last night? What the hell, Charlie thought, I've got to eat.

"OK. I have to ring my landlady first though."

"Turn right as you come out of the police station. You can't miss it. I've got a table right behind the door." They ended the call and Charlie found the bit of paper with Dilys's number and rang her.

Dilys knew exactly who he was. The word had already reached her that Charlie was without clothes or possessions.

"You're expected sweetheart, and your room is ready. I've left you some pyjamas and a shirt, and a new toothbrush and so on. The front door's open until eleven thirty."

"Pyjamas? A shirt?"

"You'd be surprised what people leave behind. Don't worry—it's all washed and ironed."

Charlie said thank you, promising to see her later.

Tom was right about it being hard to miss The Three Horseshoes. The noise of people talking at the tops of their voices spilled onto the street. A few cold-looking but animated smokers stood on the three steps up to the tall black door. The steps had black wrought iron railings, more like a smart town house than a pub, Charlie thought. But as soon as he opened the door, there was no doubt where he was.

The sound of conversation vied with the commentary from a football match on a TV screen next to the bar, and the clicks of pool being played from the far end of the room. The clientele were a mixed bag: some in suits or smart dresses, probably on their way home from work; others in jeans and sweaters; and a group of young people in a variety of paint-stained garments who were crowded round a big table and exclaiming over the deliciousness of the food at the tops of their voices. And then there was Tom, just visible near the bar. Taller and broader than everyone else, but gentle; not pushing his way through as he could so easily have done. The light over the bar caught Tom's hair, painting a bright golden stripe on the black. He looked over his shoulder to point out their table to the barmaid, and met Charlies eyes, locked onto him like a magnet with iron filings. Tom smiled. The uncomplicated smile of someone who was pleased that Charlie had arrived.

Tom waved, pointing Charlie towards a battered pine table with a bench seat close to the door. A navy-blue wool coat lay over one half of the bench, and there was a brown leather bag on the other. Charlie moved the bag and sat down, scanning the room with interest. The art students had plates of rice and curry in front of them, and were eating and talking, forks waving for emphasis. Other tables had smaller groups, but all had plates, either full or empty. The smell of food was making Charlie's mouth water, and judging from what he saw, the meal promised to be good.

A wave of exhaustion washed over Charlie, the noise and colour of the bar blurring as he gave himself permission to lean back in his seat and think about nothing. His eyes had begun to close when Tom squirmed into the bench seat next to Charlie, carefully putting two pints of lager and two sets of napkin-wrapped cutlery onto the table. Their thighs and shoulders touched, and Charlie felt a comfortable warmth in his skin where their bodies met. He had the sudden urge to lean against Tom, as if that would allow the tension of the day to dissipate. But no. Not a good idea.

Tom turned in the seat, so he could face Charlie. He'd changed out of the suit into black jeans and a dark red sweater — a half-way house between the lumberjack of the night before and the college principal of this morning. He looked good. He smelled nice—of clean clothes and Old Spice. Not that it mattered.

"Thanks for coming," Tom said. "The food comes from the Indian restaurant next door. The only choice is meat or veg, and there's only regular rice and a popadom. It's a fiver. My treat." Tom grinned.

Charlie smiled back, though even his face ached with the effects of the last twenty-four hours. "What can I say? I guess I'm a cheap date." Not that it was a date. He opened his mouth to speak again when a figure in a black apron wriggled between the tables. "Two veg?" Tom nodded and the plates were put in front of them. The curry was exactly as Tom predicted, excellent. The vegetables hadn't been boiled to mush, so he could taste peas, sweet corn and several kinds of beans, and the sauce hit the sweet spot between too hot and boring. Apart from a few compliments about the food, they ate in silence until their plates were clear, and the last bits of rice and popadoms chased until they surrendered.

"Really good," Charlie sighed, and stretched his legs out as far as he could under the table. "Thanks for suggesting it."

"I'm happy you came."

The noise level in the pub had risen, and every seat was now taken, with new arrivals pouncing as soon as anyone left. A couple of people were eyeing their empty plates, obviously wondering whether they were about to leave.

"Do you want to stay for a bit?" Tom asked. "You wanted to talk to me."

Charlie looked round. The pub was full, and the noise was loud enough that they were unlikely to be overheard. If they got more drinks, they wouldn't be interrupted by people hoping to pinch their table.

"I'll get another drink," Charlie said. He made his way to the bar through the crush and brought two more cold pints of lager back to their table. There was condensation on the sides of the glasses, making them slippery in his hands. He put them down, moisture puddling on the wood.

"I'm the bearer of bad news," he said, preparing to spoil their evening. He wished it *was* a date; just him and a nice guy getting to know one another over a couple of drinks.

11

Predator

MONDAY 7PM

"I can't tell you how we found this out, but we have reason to believe the man carrying out the assaults on your women students is still here. We think he assaulted a young woman this week."

Tom's face fell.

"But I thought everyone had been arrested?"

"Not the perpetrator, no. Look, I don't want to go all police-speak on you. I'll tell you what I know and trust you to keep it to yourself," Charlie said.

"Sure. But can I warn the students? Because I don't want any more of them hurt."

Charlie felt something inside himself melt with relief. He hadn't realised how much he had been afraid Tom would be like the others: wanting the whole mess swept under the carpet, regardless of the cost. Their discussion about Kaylan and Rico might have ended with Tom stepping up, but it had started badly.

"Damn right, you can warn the students. And we should discuss extra security, lighting, that kind of thing. But for now, I just wanted you to know that it's not over." Charlie paused. How much of the background manoeuvrings in Clwyd Police did he want to share? Enough to make Tom realise that nothing was straightforward.

"There has been a school of thought locally," he began, "about whether flashing, or even masturbating in public is a sexual assault."

"Of course it bloody is. And anyway, isn't it the beginning of something worse?" Tom was angry.

"I agree with you, and even if I didn't, the law is clear— it's an assault. Those women were made to watch something they didn't want to see, and they watched because they were threatened with something worse. You're right that flashers do escalate. We should have taken this much more seriously from day one." Charlie threw up his hands. "It's too late for that. We have to catch him before he does it again." Tom nodded vigorously.

"You know what?" Tom said, pulling his coat from the back of the bench. "Jess from the Student Union has a list. I went to see her today after I'd spoken to you, and she showed me. Most of the attacks happened after dark, on the college campus. I'm going to take a walk round, just in case."

Charlie put his hand on Tom's arm. "Hang on, don't you have security?"

"One Campus Services Officer at night, and he only goes outside if he hears an alarm. We were told it wasn't real, remember." Tom's face hardened. "And my predecessors were still dithering about whether the cost of extra lighting and CCTV was worth it. We need a police presence."

"Tell me about it," muttered Charlie. "If you're going, I'm coming with you." Because Tom was a big guy, but the flasher carried a knife and wasn't afraid to use it.

AFTER THE NOISE and life in the pub, the streets outside were quiet. Charlie was glad of his hi-vis jacket, pulling it more tightly around himself to keep out the chill. He envied Tom his wool pea coat, and envied him still more when he produced a knitted scarf from his pocket. It hadn't seemed particularly cold earlier in the day, but now the sun had gone the temperature had dropped. Charlie was tired, and he knew that made him feel colder. He shivered.

"You OK?" Tom asked.

"It's been a long day," Charlie said, feeling every moment of the long day in his bones.

The front of the art college was floodlit, casting dark shadows around the walls and in front of the now closed doors.

"None of the attacks happened in the courtyard," Tom said. "It's locked quite early, though a few of the studios and workshops are open, and of course the library is open late — but that's got its own outside door. Staff have keys, so they can get in and out of the main building if they need to."

Charlie shivered again. He didn't like the idea of being alone in the college. He knew, rationally, that there were a few hundred students nearby, using the library or in the halls of residence, but it seemed spooky and deserted. The paths were all lit by bollards, giving just enough light for them to see the path, but nothing beyond it. A few lampposts showed the gateway to the road and the path to the library, which took up a corner of the main building, with its own outside entrance.

"No one's sketching piles of leaves at night, then," he asked.

Tom laughed. "We do make the poor buggers suffer. But everything rests on drawing. Drawing is the foundation. Even Vitruvious agrees with that. It's one of the *only* things we agree about."

"Is he really called Inigo Vitruvious?"

Tom laughed again. "I shouldn't think so for a minute. On the other hand, he lives in a big house in a nice village, so I guess he comes from money. Rich people can call their kids anything. He's been here almost as long as I have and I've never heard him called anything else."

"But you don't actually know?"

"Art colleges are peculiar places. Everyone wants to be successful, and for the college itself to be successful because that reflects on them, but no one wants success for their colleagues. So V might well have chosen a bizarre name for himself to get more attention. Or maybe it's his actual name. I suppose I could find out, now I'm allegedly in charge." Tom shrugged. "There is more jealousy in a place like this than in any group of teenage girls."

"Is Vitruvious successful?"

Tom paused. Away from the floodlights, Charlie could see a half moon caught between drifting clouds. He looked down. Dead leaves edged the path, smelling of damp earth, all colour turned to shades of grey. He realised that in the last few minutes he'd stopped wanting answers to his policeman's questions, and begun wanting to hear about Tom's world.

"V is *noticed*. Mainly because he does the angry lefty artist so well. Maybe it's the name too. Pontificates at the drop of a hat about the role of class society in the history of art. He has an agent whose job is to get him on TV as often as he can. The thing is that he's an extremely good painter. He has been painting seascapes and portraits of refugees for a few years now. I'll show you. He can't just be dismissed as a posturing fool, tempting though it is."

Tom turned and headed back the way they had come, until they reached a door set into the college wall. "Back of the library," Tom said. The lock was operated by an electronic fob and opened with a beep, and they stepped into what looked like a storeroom. Charlie looked round. Stacking chairs and folding tables took up most of the space, together with cardboard boxes. Tom waved at them.

"This may be the computer age," he said, "but we still send out mountains of paper. Look, this is what I wanted you to see." Charlie saw that one side of the room had pictures leaning against it, some turned to face the wall, others covered with hessian sheets. Tom lifted a hessian sheet and moved the painting to lean against the cardboard boxes.

It was about four or five feet square, dominating the space. Charlie had an impression of a mass of blues and greens, appearing to move in some kind of rhythm. Blobs of other colours appeared woven amongst them. Tom took Charlie's arm and pulled him as far away from the canvas as they could get, and the image resolved itself. Human bodies being washed around in a wild sea. Limbs and heads appearing above the waves, or showing as shadows under the restless water. There was no shore, and no horizon. Just the ocean, and the bodies. In the corner, two letters, IV.

"Wow," Charlie said, "not something I'd want in my living room."

"Indeed. Not many people do. Paintings on this scale don't sell, and so far no one's offering him an exhibition space that he thinks is worthy of them. He can be his own worst enemy. Anyway. I wanted you to see some of his work, before you dismiss him as the idiot he undoubtedly is."

They left the storeroom and retraced their steps.

"Do you see both sides of everything?" Charlie asked. They had come to a standstill in the half light. Young trees moved against their stakes in a light breeze, and Charlie could taste woodsmoke in the air.

Tom shrugged. "I wasn't aware that I did."

"Take it from me. Are *you* successful? Yes or no."

"Yes or no?"

"No caveats, no context, yes or no."

"Then, yes."

The faint rustling from the trees stopped and the moon disappeared behind a cloud. Charlie smelled Old Spice and wool and held his breath. The air between them crackled.

Then the library door opened with a splash of light and a burst of conversation, and the moment passed.

The narrow windows of the halls of residence spilled different coloured lights.

"Can I ask why you were in New York?" Charlie asked. He wanted to know, but he also wanted to keep Tom talking. Was he flirting? He didn't think so. Tom was simply interesting. He heard the smile in Tom's voice as he answered.

"New York was me *being successful*. I got a major grant from an arts foundation to stay there for six months and produce any work I liked. The foundation provided me with a flat, and a generous stipend, and when I got back, whatever I made would have sold for good money. Success. Except I had to come back and pretend to run the college. Which might look like success. At least in New York I knew what I was doing."

"What do you paint?"

"Paint! I don't *paint*. I'm a printmaker. Dear God, paint?"

Charlie had only the vaguest notion of what a printmaker made. Prints, obviously. Etchings? He would find out.

Students in twos and threes were making their way from the library towards the main entrance to the residence building. Tom looked at his watch.

"The library is closing. Library staff will be around for half an hour or so, and this area is well-lit. We should have a look around the back." He led the way past the door to the library and into the darkness beyond. The paths had the dim bollard lights, but all the windows in the main building were dark. Charlie could see the expanse of mostly empty car park to the left, and to the right, a cluster of sheds, containers and portacabins looming out of the darkness, barely visible against the night sky.

"Storage, and places to make things too big or messy for the studios in the main building." Tom said. "The ceramics people build fires and dig holes ..." Charlie found out about the holes by falling into one of them. For the second time in twenty-four hours, Charlie felt Tom's arms holding him upright, and this time he didn't mind so much. He minded the scrapes on his hands, but he felt fine being close to Tom. Except this was exactly what he needed to avoid. Llanfair was already struggling to recover from the corrupt collusion between college and police. They needed to co-operate, for the sake of Tom's students and Charlie and his colleagues' jobs, but there was a line. It was bright red, Charlie knew where it was, and he wasn't going to cross it. So he stepped out of Tom's embrace and said thank you for picking him up.

"But I can't believe there's anyone lurking amongst this lot," he said. "Our flasher might be hiding here, but if any student was working late, we'd see the lights. Get the warning out tomorrow, but I think we've done enough for tonight."

"You're the expert," Tom said, not sounding entirely convinced. "Where are you staying?"

"With Eddy's Aunty Dilys," Charlie said without thinking. He'd forgotten the name of the house, or the street; the guest house had become Aunty Dilys's in his mind.

"I'll walk you back," Tom said. "I'm going to assume there aren't two guest houses run by someone called Dilys. That's where we put our visitors. We get a few raised eyebrows, but her beds are comfortable, it's spotless and the breakfasts are a feast. Dilys loves her work, and it shows."

"My parents run a bed and breakfast in Holyhead," Charlie said, "and it's the complete opposite. My mother hates it, everything about it." He didn't know why he'd told Tom that. Not the bed and breakfast, that wasn't a shameful profession. They weren't smugglers or drug dealers. It was the bit about his mother. He'd never seen it so clearly before, and it felt good to get the words into the open.

"That must have been hard to live with," Tom said, and he was too close again, overwhelming Charlie's senses with his gentle voice, his size and his scent. But Charlie stayed on the right side of the line.

"My mother could disapprove for Wales," Charlie said, because it was true, if hardly relevant. "I need to get some sleep. We haven't even talked about your missing student yet."

"Tomorrow," Tom said. "It can all wait until tomorrow."

Charlie had the strong sense that it couldn't wait, but if he didn't get some sleep, his brain was going to shut down.

"Can I call you in the morning?" he asked Tom.

"Please do."

Without Charlie noticing, Tom had led him from the college, down a narrow lane and back into the big car park. He took Charlie's arm gently, as if recognising that Charlie's ability to process information had now left the building. "It's just down here." They stopped on the street outside a house with a tiny front garden. The railings and front door were painted in a glossy black, shiny under the streetlights.

"Dilys's place," Tom said.

It was like being delivered home after a date. Except it hadn't been a date, and the urge he had to kiss Tom good-night was on the wrong side of the red line.

"Thanks," he said.

The door opened and a woman's face peered out. She saw Tom and smiled. "You must be Charlie Rees," she said. "I was about to lock up when I heard you talking." The woman was tiny, probably in her sixties, dressed in leggings and a T-shirt despite the cold. She had dyed her hair electric blue, and her face fell naturally into a smile. "Come on in."

Tom touched Charlie's arm. "We'll speak tomorrow," he said and walked away.

CHARLIE HAD the vague impression of a small room, with an even smaller bathroom, tucked into the back of the house. Dilys had hustled him through the hallway, flinging open a door to the residents' lounge, "Where you can always make a drink," pointing through an archway, "breakfast," and up the thickly carpeted stairs and into his room. He couldn't bring himself to climb into those pristine white sheets without a shower, especially when Dilys pointed out a small pile of clothes on the armchair. On top were a set of brightly coloured pyjamas, decorated with dragons.

"Help yourself," Dilys said. "All clean and pressed. Most of it's nearly new. And while we're on the subject of clothes, I know the courier for Marks and Spencers and he's agreed to come here first thing, not to the cop shop. So, new clothes before breakfast." She gave a quick grin. "Right then, I'll see you in the morning."

The shower was bliss. The dragon pyjamas fitted, and the bed was as comfortable as promised by Tom. The promise of Tom… That was Charlie's last thought before he fell asleep.

12

The detective's new clothes
TUESDAY 6.55AM

Charlie woke to the sound of someone knocking at the door to his room.

"Only me!" Dilys called.

Charlie stumbled the short step to the door and opened it. Dilys held three sealed plastic bags. He took them from her, all his limbs stiff from sleeping so soundly that he woke up in the same position he'd gone to sleep in.

"Love those pyjamas," Dilys said. "You should keep them. What time for breakfast?"

Charlie rubbed his eyes.

"What time is it now?"

"Just before seven."

"Half an hour then. And Dilys? Is it OK to call you that?" she nodded. "Can I stay here for a few more days? Or do you need the room?"

"Stay as long as you like, sweetheart. I've already got you pencilled in for a week." Then she was gone, and he heard her running down the stairs.

Charlie collapsed back on to the bed. He didn't want to wake up and face the day, not without another three or four hours sleep. But the to-do list was longer every time he looked at it, and there were only four of them to do it.

He opened all the plastic bags and looked at the clothes with some relief. He was going to be wearing jeans and sweaters rather than a suit, but no way was he ordering a suit online. Best of all, he now had a warm coat.

He showered and shaved at warp speed, got dressed and was peering through the archway by seven-thirty. He was tired, but he was comfortable, and his head was clear.

THE BREAKFAST WAS everything promised by Tom. There were four small wooden tables laid with startlingly white tablecloths. Only one was laid for service, with white china, though another had coffee drips and crumbs showing where someone had already eaten. There was a small table bearing cereal, tea bags, an urn of hot water and jugs of orange juice and milk. The coffee machine was one Charlie had been lusting after for some time. He put one of the little pods into its slot and pressed the button. The coffee was hot and strong, with a layer of *crema* covering the surface. He vowed to drink it quickly so there would be time for another. Charlie helped himself to orange juice. The two drinks alone would finish the job of waking him up.

When Dilys asked him what he wanted for 'proper breakfast' he remembered Hayden the day before.

"What I would really like is a bacon sandwich," he said. Dilys grinned. It seemed to be her default expression.

"Coming up," she said and disappeared through a door into what must be the kitchen.

If anything, the bacon sandwich was even better than Hayden's.

He couldn't imagine his mother making bacon sandwiches at the whim of a guest. She offered a Full Breakfast, take it or leave it. Requests for no mushrooms or an extra tomato were always fulfilled, but with pursed lips and an icy stare. Yet a bacon sandwich was much less effort than the combination of items his mother insisted on cooking. Anything uneaten was regarded as a personal affront. Charlie shook his head. If his mother wanted to martyr herself, that was her choice, and he had work to do. He left his crusts, because he knew Dilys wouldn't mind. She'd just put them out for the birds. It was a tiny act of rebellion against his mother's disapproval, but it felt good. Some people get on top of this stuff when they're still teenagers, he thought, but then those people don't have to deal with my mother.

AT THE POLICE STATION, Charlie found Eddy staring at the video of the assault. Charlie looked over his shoulder. There was a pop-up box in the corner of the screen. It looked like a newspaper headline. Eddy minimised it before Charlie could read what it said.

"If we could get an image of the bloke, we could show it to the other victims and see if it's the same guy. I don't have the skills to do it, but I know a woman who does."

"I'd like the image, but I'm not sure about showing it to the other victims." Charlie said, "No, what we need is to show it round the college and the town. Someone knows who it is. So can you get this woman to work her magic?"

"Sorry, Sarge, you'll have to ask DCI Ravensbourne. It'd be better coming from you." Charlie didn't see how it could make a difference, but he took the number anyway.

"I'm going over to the college," Charlie said. "I want to check that the students have been warned, and I'll have another go at Kaylan." Eddy opened his mouth to speak, and Charlie held up a hand to stop him.

"I want you to check whether there is any possibility that his story is true. That he could have lost a week of his life. Natural causes, drugs, concussion, look at them all."

"Tell me you don't believe that load of bullshit."

"That isn't the point. We have to check."

Eddy turned away.

"Eddy. We have to check. And while you're checking, could you find out everything you can about Harrington-Bowen? Because I still don't know whether he left those videos by mistake, or someone planted them."

This time Eddy nodded, though the camaraderie they'd enjoyed yesterday seemed to have departed. Out of the corner of his eye, Charlie saw another pop-up appear in Eddy's screen. Again, Eddy minimised it, before saying,

"We also need to get a bead on the gardener's apprentice. Mags and Patsy were supposed to have a look for him yesterday, but I don't know how far they got. See if he was Molotov cocktail guy. The fire brigade might be worth another call, too."

"Stick it on the list."

"What about you, Sarge?"

"I'm hoping that if I see Kaylan on his own, on his own turf so to speak, he might be more forthcoming. I also want to talk to Vitruvious. Something about that guy doesn't ring true."

"You ask me, none of that art college crowd ring true. I wouldn't trust any of them."

"We can trust Tom. He wasn't here." Charlie said what he was thinking and got a snort of disdain from Eddy.

"All right for him to go swanning off to New York. Obviously wasn't worried about leaving his teenage daughters behind with a pervert on the loose. So, either he didn't care about his family, or he didn't believe those women who reported assaults. Some father he is."

Charlie hoped the shock didn't show on his face. He had met Tom in a gay bar, where he appeared to be well known. Tom had wanted to kiss him last night, Charlie was sure of it, and he'd definitely tried to pick Charlie up in the bar. Tom had appeared genuinely anxious about the women students on campus—worried enough to visit the student's Union, and worried enough to want to walk round the college after dark. But if he was a family man playing away from home, what else had he been lying about?

KAYLAN'S ROOM in the hall of residence was still a mess, just a re-arranged mess. The mess that had been piled up on the chairs was now scattered all over the floor. The art materials on the desk had been pushed to one side, in favour of an expensive laptop.

"The cleaners come on a Thursday. Wednesday night I pick it up. It's mostly OK until the weekend," he said, turfing a pile of miscellaneous items from the easy chair onto the floor. "Have a seat." Kaylan himself sat on the un-made bed and pulled his knees into his chest, wrapping his arms around them.

"It's not very big, this place," Charlie said to break the ice.

"Not very big, unbelievably expensive, but at least I don't have a roommate. All the places I looked at in the US were shared."

"So why come here?"

Kaylan unwound one hand from his knees, and used the fingers to number off his reasons.

"It's actually pretty cheap compared to home. It's in the UK, and who wouldn't want to study here? There's easy access to Paris, and Rome, London…" Charlie wondered whether Kaylan had checked exactly how long those trips took from rural north Wales, or if he'd just taken the college website at face value. "But number one was coming to study with Vitruvious. In the States, someone like him would only teach graduate students. Here he teaches everyone."

"I saw," Charlie remembered the exhortation to *look, really look*, at the wall of the main building.

Then Kaylan broke into a big smile. Not one of the innocent smiles Charlie had had from Dilys over breakfast. This smile had echoes of anger and even hatred.

"The best thing about Vitruvious is that my parents hate him. They voted for Trump, and they pretend they believe the 2020 election was stolen. They don't; they're just racists, who make more money under a right-wing federal government."

"You're spending your parents' money on supporting someone who disagrees with everything they believe in?"

Kaylan smiled the unpleasant sneering smile again.

"God, no. They would have refused to pay. This is my own money, from my grandparents. I inherited when I was eighteen. They can't stop me spending it on coming here."

Charlie kept his face neutral as he considered Kaylan's use of the phrase *my own money* used as if he were talking about any other possession. Enough money to pay the costs of a three-year degree in a foreign country. No wonder Kaylan was arrogant. He made a mental note to ask Tom about the costs for someone like Kaylan before remembering that Tom was potentially a liar.

"Having Vetruvious as your tutor was your main motivation? But he didn't make any kind of fuss when you disappeared." Charlie wanted to see Kaylan's reaction to the idea that his hero might not have noticed him, Kaylan. That Vitruvious didn't care enough about his students that their absence registered.

"But, he knew…" Kaylan bit back the rest of the sentence, and continued, "he knew lots of new students get ill. He wouldn't have worried. Not straight away. All the tutors talked about freshers' flu, and not coming to classes if we were unwell. Just courtesy to the rest of the class …" Kaylan was gabbling, words tumbling out. In an attempt to hide what he'd begun to say?

"You said *he knew*. Did Vitruvious know where you were? Kaylan?"

"How could he know where I was? I didn't know. You're being ridiculous."

The arms were back round Kaylan's knees, hugging tightly, his body closed in on itself, as if to repel questions he didn't want to hear.

Charlie tried again. He sat back in the chair and kept his voice as gentle as he could. "Some things about your story don't make sense, Kaylan. Is there some medical condition we should know about? Have you lost big chunks of time before?"

"No! I just don't know, OK."

"Did you perhaps take something... maybe without even knowing about it...? Some drugs can cause memory loss." Charlie knew this was true, though he never heard of anyone losing their memory for a week, not from the kind of drugs available on the streets of a small Welsh town.

"No. I said *no*. I don't know what happened or why. I just want to get on with my classes. I don't want to talk to you any more. I don't have to talk to you, or has this turned into a police state without me noticing?"

Charlie stood up, managing not to slide on the crisp packets under his feet.

"No, you don't have to talk to me. But Rico is still missing. I've been a police officer long enough to know when I'm not being told the full story. I'm glad you're back, but I'm not going to stop asking questions until Rico is back, too."

13

Unwelcome confrontation
TUESDAY 10AM

Tom was wearing another three-piece suit, this one in a very faint pin-striped navy blue. His tie was the colour Charlie's mother called 'shocking pink'. Not a colour she approved of. Charlie was prepared to approve of it on Tom, before reminding himself that Tom had lied. Or if not lied, at least not told the whole truth. Like Kaylan. Except while Kaylan had immediately rung his alarm bells, Tom had appeared sincere. Not that it was any of his business whether Tom was a married family man, though it would make it easier to turn down his offers of dinner.

"Charlie?" Tom said.

"Sorry, woolgathering. I came to see whether you had been able to warn the students." And to find out more about Vitruvious, but that could wait for a bit.

"I did," Tom said. "We have some kind of software that sends them all a text message. Here." He opened his laptop and swivelled it around to face Charlie. The message read:

From Dr Tomos Pennant, Acting Principal

We have been informed by the local police that there may be further assaults on women students. We urge students to be vigilant at all times. The college will be increasing patrols around the campus after dark from tonight. Please report **anything** *suspicious to my secretary (Ms Ann Hathersage, room 2.1a) or to the Students' Union.*

"That is certainly a turnaround from your predecessor's messages." Charlie said.

"You convinced me," Tom said. "You and that young woman in the Students' Union. I was too tied up in having been dragged back from New York and made to do this job. I'd bought in to the whole 'protect the college's reputation' thing. But there's no point trying to protect the college at the expense of our students." He sighed. "Sorry, thinking aloud."

"Where are you getting the staff to patrol the college?" Charlie asked.

"Changing the shift patterns for the existing Campus Services Officers. Except … how do I know I'm not sending the flasher to patrol the campus?" Tom looked worried. "We don't have enough people to pair them up. I don't know who I can trust. And another thing. I walked round again last night after I took you to Dilys's. I'm sure there was someone else there. Between the library entrance and the workshops, where it's really dark." He rested his elbows on the desk and put his head in his hands. "Shit, Charlie. I have no idea what I'm doing here." He massaged the lines on his forehead with long fingers and pushed his dark hair back behind his ears.

"You said the Students' Union had been helpful. Could you pay them to patrol—in pairs? With big torches, and alarms?"

"Yes. Yes we can," Tom said. "I'll go over there now."

Charlie privately resolved that either he, or one of the other of their tiny crew would walk round the campus, and the streets close to it, every evening if they possibly could. But best of all would be to catch the bastard before he hurt someone else.

Tom pushed his chair back, obviously impatient to visit the Students' Union.

"You still have a missing student," Charlie said. "Kaylan is back, but Rico is still missing." Tom deflated and put his head back in his hands.

"I told you I shouldn't be doing this job. I'd forgotten all about them."

Charlie described how they had been called to Brocklehurst and collected Kaylan from the hospital. Tom lifted his head at Brocklehurst, but when Charlie asked him about it, he shrugged. "It's one of those arty places, I think. Maybe someone on the staff lives there."

"Kaylan says he doesn't remember anything between being in his room here, and walking into the police station in Brocklehurst a week later. When he first went to the police, he said that he thought Rico was dead. But when he talked to us, he said he couldn't remember."

"You don't believe him?"

"I'm a policeman. I don't believe anything unless I have evidence. Which is why I want to see the personnel files for everyone who works here. And when I've gone through those, we'll start on the students."

"You can't."

"I can if you help me. Or I can get a warrant, which will take time, during which time Rico is still missing, and your students are in danger. What's it to be?"

"Staff records are confidential. All kinds of private information could be there. Illnesses. Divorce. Disciplinary stuff, I don't know. How do we know we can trust you after what's happened?"

Anger rose up in Charlie's throat like bile. Tom's eyes were wide across the desk, and Charlie caught them, staring back.

"We are probably the only people you can trust. None of us attacked those women or tried to cover it up. And you know what? Everyone lies to us. Everyone. I'm assuming there will be some truth in your records, which is why I want to see them."

Tom stood up and began to pace up and down the office,

ignoring Charlie. Tom's hands moved constantly: making fists then banging them together, waving his arms, and pacing, pacing, as his mind worked.

"You can come here," he said eventually. "Use our computers, right here in this office. No printing, no emailing, no data sticks, just notes. Take it or leave it. But you'll need a warrant for the students. I might get away with the staff, but no chance with the students."

He stopped in front of Charlie, looking down, calmer now, eyes softer. He pushed the hair back behind his ears, and a slight flush rose on his cheeks. "I haven't lied to you, Charlie. But I have had this." He turned his laptop round to face Charlie again and clicked in the corner. The same pop-up box that Charlie had seen on Eddy's computer appeared. This time he could read what it said:

*Exclusive: **Sun, sex and murder! Gay cop's holiday hook-up ends in murder trial.*** There was a picture of a slender man in a suit and sunglasses walking into a Spanish court.

"That's you," Tom said.

Charlie had been towered over by scarier men than Tom, so he didn't move.

"I did nothing wrong; I was a witness. I slept with a man, and a few days later he was arrested for murder." Charlie said. "I don't know where you got this. It's also been all over the tabloid press, so I can hardly pretend it didn't happen. But you tried to pick me up in a gay bar, and offered me dinner, like it was a date. And somehow forgot to mention your wife and children."

Tom sank onto his haunches in front of Charlie, so it was his turn to look up.

"Charlie, I have children. I'm not ashamed of them. It's complicated." As he opened his mouth to continue, the quiet of the college was shattered by a piercing scream, and then another, and the sound of feet pounding along corridors and down stairs.

Charlie looked out of the window. Students were huddled together gesticulating wildly, pointing to the library or possibly the workshops beyond. He ran for the stairs and the court-yard, Tom on his heels. The screams were definitely coming from behind the main building.

"This way," Tom pulled him through a door off the court-yard and into the main building, along a corridor and then out through a fire door into the cluster of workshops and storage containers. A campus services officer stood by the door to one of the sheds, holding on to the screamer, a middle-aged woman in jeans and a long white shirt.

The smell of decomposition filled Charlie's nose. Like everything rotten in the world, all at once.

"Tom, Tom, oh God, it's horrible." The screamer had thrown herself at Tom.

"What is it, Violet?" Tom asked, holding onto the woman as she continued to wail.

"It's a boy. A dead boy. In my studio, oh God."

Charlie had a horrible feeling he knew who it was. He showed his warrant card to the campus officer and told him to keep everyone as far away from the building as he could. Then he took a deep breath and opened the door, trying not to gag.

THE WORKSHOP, or studio or whatever Violet had called it, was full of junk. Every kind of junk, from old furniture to broken crockery, children's toys, boxes of nails, telephone directories, door handles. He thought there might have been some order to it, but he was too busy trying to locate the source of the smell. He found it in the furthest corner, obviously a work-space. The artist had been making a bed from planks of wood, decorated by old toys and children's picture books. There might have been a few broken christening mugs amongst it. Charlie concentrated on the details of the bed, rather than on the figure laid carefully upon it.

The body was naked, bloated and discoloured, and the smell of putrefaction filled the air. But Charlie could see the brown hair and tattoo of a tree and had no doubt he was looking at the earthly remains of Rico Pepperdine. He was no forensic scientist, but this body was a few days old, and the case would be out of his hands now. All he could do was secure the scene and call for help. He cast his eyes around, but if there were physical clues, they would be indistinguishable from the mountains of junk.

He reached for his phone, unsure who to call, so he started with Eddy.

"We've found Rico. In some workshop full of junk at the college. He's dead. Been dead for days. We need the whole circus, and we need to secure the scene and start taking names. You all get down here and I'll call Kent."

A string of swear words came out of Charlie's phone. "Kent's on indefinite leave. We just got an email," Eddy said, "They haven't used the word suspended, but they're trying to make him take the fall for everything that's gone wrong in Llanfair. Ring DCI Ravensbourne. I trust her."

"You know her, you ring her. Ask her to give me a call straight away. We need an experienced SIO, so do it now."

Charlie walked out of the workshop, hands in his pockets, careful not to touch anything. Once outside, he closed the door, lessening the smell, though not getting rid of it alto-gether. He was pleased to see that the screaming Violet had gone, with the campus services officer, leaving Tom with his arms wrapped round himself and his chin almost resting on his chest. There was an autumn chill to the air, and the sky had clouded over to a uniform dull grey. This was a day to be inside with the fire on, not to be standing around, coatless, knowing that a young man was dead nearby.

When Charlie appeared, Tom straightened up. "I sent Violet to have a cup of tea. I hope that's OK? Can you tell me anything?" Tom said.

"I can tell you that there is a young man's body in the workshop. Beyond that, I don't know. I've asked everyone from the police station to come down here. We're going to have to close this whole area." Despite the lies, Charlie still had the urge to confide in Tom, glad he had waited behind. But Tom was the college principal. Of course he would want to know what was happening.

"What can I do to help?" Tom asked.

Charlie sighed. There would be major disruption to college life, and the tiny amount of progress the four of them had made would disappear in a puff of smoke.

"Nothing, yet," he said. "We need to make sure all these sheds and workshops are closed, and depending on what the SIO says, the college may have to close. Sorry, Senior Investigating Officer. Not me. I'm waiting for a call."

They stood in silence for a moment. Then Tom said, "Is this going to be bad for you? That it's happened on your watch?"

The concern was genuine, Charlie would have sworn it was. The answer would be *yes* it will be bad. Probably worse than bad. Because the pressure is always worse for a suspicious death, and the media were already watching. But the same was true for Tom. He was principal of the college, and in his brief tenure, had lost two students and found one of them dead. That was apart from the ongoing assaults on women students. He wanted to say some of this when his phone rang.

"Charlie Rees? This is DCI Freya Ravensbourne. I'll be there in an hour. I've called Hector Powell, the pathologist, and he's on his way. Scenes of crime officers will follow as soon as they can. I'm told you know what you're doing, so please get on with doing it."

"Yes, ma'am," Charlie said, feeling weights lift from his shoulders.

"Get the scene secure and start looking for witnesses. I'll see you soon."

The ground seemed to steady beneath Charlie's feet. The police service is a hierarchical organisation—you do what you're told, go where you're sent. Charlie had followed his orders to the best of his ability. But he couldn't help the sense of relief that from here on, what he had to do were the familiar tasks of being a sergeant while someone else took responsibility. Even better, he looked up to see Eddy, Mags and Patsy picking their way through the debris around the sheds. Patsy carried a roll of police tape, and Eddy had a bunch of stakes under his arm. It was a mess, but at least now he wasn't the only one trying to clear it up.

14

Freya

TUESDAY 2PM

From the transcript of a court case somewhere in Spain*

*English translation

Attorney for the Prosecution (AP): Is it your testimony that you spent the night with the defendant?

Witness: Yes, sir.

AP: Having spent the previous evening in a bar for homosexual men, having a drunk a great deal of alcohol?

Witness: Yes, sir.

AP: And isn't it true that you had never met the defendant until that night?

Witness: Yes, it is true.

AP: Would the term for your relationship with the defendant be "hook up"?

Witness: Possibly. I wouldn't argue with it.

AP: To sum up. You picked up a man you had never met before, had a great deal to drink and took him back to your hotel room, where you had sex and presumably fell asleep. Is that what happened?

Witness: Yes, sir.

AP: In your statement to the police, you insisted that the

defendant had been with you all night. I believe your words were, "I would have heard if he'd got up to murder someone." Is that what you said?

Witness: Yes, sir.

AP: On reflection, would you stand by that statement?

Witness: In the light of later events, I may have been mistaken.

DCI FREYA RAVENSBOURNE was a remarkably untidy woman. She was the first to arrive, beating pathologist Hector Powell and the team of forensic investigators. Ravensbourne came in a marked car, with a uniformed driver, and when she got out she showered the ground with crumbs and chocolate wrappers. The wrappers she carefully picked up, and handed to the driver. Her brown hair was streaked with grey and looked as if it had been last brushed several weeks before. Her black trousers were frayed around the bottom, and her lime green padded jacket leaked padding. But her eyes were sharp, and her head turned this way and that, taking everything in, looking at the walls of the main building and then the less salubrious sheds and workshops. She sniffed the air, foul with decay.

The whole area from the car park through to the fire door Tom had used had been taped off. All the sheds and workshops were inside the tape, some of their users having left under protest. As a precaution, Charlie had asked Tom to close those sections of corridor and offices overlooking the crime scene. If they needed to, Forensics could erect a tent, not least to hide moving the body. In the meantime, no one could watch what was happening.

Charlie stepped forwards. "Ma'am," he said, "I'm DS Charlie Rees."

She smiled, showing uneven teeth stained by tobacco, the smell of which came from her clothes. "Charlie, call me boss.

Save ma'am for when you meet royalty." She gripped his arm and all but frogmarched him back to the car. "Take a walk, Etheridge," she said. The uniformed constable exited the car with a nod, and opened the back door for Charlie. She slid in next to him. "Chewing gum?" Ravensbourne asked, fishing a packet out of her trouser pocket. Charlie shook his head. "Better than smoking, or so I'm told," she said.

"I don't smoke either, ma … boss."

"Don't suppose you do, working for clean-living Kent." She laughed and smacked his arm, hard enough to bruise. "Don't take me seriously. Mal and I are old friends." Her voice changed, and this time, it matched the sharp eyes. "Mal Kent has been suspended in all but name. They won't get anywhere with it, but the big cheeses have got it into their heads that they can blame him for everything that went wrong here. That way, no one will look too closely at what they were doing for the last six months. It took them a while to get the courage to call him in, so they're all relaxed now, and not concentrating properly. They *think* they can start slipping their friends back into the job, with Kent out of the way. But we don't want that, do we Charlie?"

"Do you mean reinstating the officers suspended from Llanfair?" Charlie asked.

Ravensbourne nodded, sharply.

"Then, no," Charlie said, "But this is different—this murder, or whatever. And the assaults are still going on, or rather we think there has been another one. The police station was attacked—did you know about that?" Charlie heard his own voice rising as some of the panic from the last thirty-six hours leaked out.

"Deep breath, Charlie, and tell me everything, in order please. We've got about ten minutes, max, before the circus arrives."

Charlie took a deep breath and told her.

She produced a tiny police-issue notebook and a pencil and made the occasional scribble.

"So," she said, when Charlie had finished. "Harrington-Bowen is either dirtier than we thought, or someone just as dirty has got it in for him, and planted that video. The college has been so focussed on keeping its reputation so it can attract foreign students who pay the biggest fees, that it was easy pickings for a bunch of officers who don't know the law—or were protecting someone they knew. The new guy, Tom Pennant, didn't pay any attention to the two missing students because a, he didn't want the job, and b, until you came along, he bought into the whole *protect the college* thing. One of the missing students is back, and his story has more holes than my gardening trousers, and the other one is lying dead in that workshop. Then one of your officers thinks the flasher is still doing *his* thing, and finally, someone attacked the police station."

Charlie remembered the fake email from superintendent Kent, and told Ravensbourne.

"Anything else?" she asked, but there was kindness in her voice.

He shook his head. There was bound to have been something he'd forgotten, but he thought this extraordinary woman would probably forgive him when he remembered what it was.

"You've done well," she said. "I want you to concentrate on the kid who came back. I can tell you've got a few ideas about this Vitruvius bloke. Follow your hunch. Check with Kaylan's parents that what he told you is true. Get Eddy on to Molotov cocktail man. You've got witnesses and a description. We can grab that little scrote at least. Van was stolen locally, and I'd bet on the thief being a local. I'll get the video of our flasher enhanced as much as I can. I need your two other officers looking for witnesses here." Charlie thought there was more to come, but a battered Volvo pulled in next to them, managing to park across two spaces, and a familiar figure got out: Hector Powell, pathologist.

Ravensbourne gripped Charlie's arm again. "Before you do anything, I need you in there with Hector and the body. If it's looking like this Rico kid, I'm going to want you to ring the parents for dental records, DNA or whatever." Having given him the worst job of the day, she pulled her chewing gum out again and unpacked another stick. "Sure you don't want some?"

It wouldn't help with the smell, he knew that. Nothing did.

It was after two o'clock when Charlie got the nod to ring the Pepperdines in Los Angeles. The body, almost certainly Rico, had been removed, and Hector Powell had followed, narrowly missing the gate posts to the car park. He had told Charlie that the body had been moved after death, which he could tell by the settlement of the blood … or something, Charlie didn't want to look too closely. The pathologist had no theories as to the cause of death, promising only to complete the post-mortem as quickly as possible.

Charlie walked out of the reeking workshop with Hector.

"You know Mal has been sent home?" Hector asked.

Charlie nodded.

"None of my business, of course. I'm only a humble pathologist, but God, Charlie, this whole business stinks, and I don't just mean our friend back there."

Charlie didn't know Hector well, but he was a familiar face. "Have you worked with DCI Ravensbourne before?" he asked. What he wanted to know was *can I trust her?* Thankfully, Hector got the sub-text.

"I have, and she's great. The case is in good hands." He smiled and gave Charlie a pat on the arm, which Charlie found oddly reassuring. "You don't need to hang around for the next bit," he said. "Moving this poor chap is not going to be fun. You should ask your scenes of crime bods to look for a tarpaulin, or similar, because they would have needed it to get him here."

Charlie told Ravensbourne, and soon the forensics teams were crawling over the workshop. When they'd done, Violet would be invited back to see if anything appeared out of place.

Charlie went back to the police station to call Kaylan's parents, His father had already left for work, but Mrs Sully was at home, and more than willing to talk to a Welsh police-man. Charlie had the feeling that she would have talked to anyone, especially about her son.

"He's an *only*, yanno, and that makes them different, don't you think? No sibs to rub off the corners, my mom used to say, rest her soul. Cancer. Wouldn't see the doctor. She left him all that money, too much for someone like Kaylan. Defiance. It's a disorder. He can't help it. Though I don't care what he's done. He's my child, and I'll always stand by him."

Every now and then, Charlie squeezed a question in, but in truth he didn't need to. The upset caused by Kaylan's deci-sion to spend his grandmother's money on studying with Vitruvious was close to the surface. Charlie did manage to establish that there had been contact between Vitruvious and Kaylan before he left Chicago, but in general, Kaylan's mother seemed to Charlie like a caricature. "Refugees," she said. "He kept talking about refugees. I told him, we need to keep American jobs for Americans. That's why President Trump built the wall, you know. You should have a wall. Keep them out." She blamed "the gays" for something, possibly Covid, and gave him a brief rehearsal of the "great replacement theory" which apparently a conspiracy to replace white people with people of colour. Charlie wanted to argue but he recognised that it would be a waste of breath. No one who could espouse such nonsense was going to be receptive to a dose of reality. The racist theories were interspersed with Mrs Sully extolling the virtues of the many excellent art colleges in the greater Chicago area. Individually, by name, and in detail. "Except I never knew he was all that good at art, which just goes to show. I thought he'd go into computers, like his poppa. Biggest cyber-security consultants in the mid-west. His teachers said he was good at computers. But he gets an idea in his head, and there's no shifting it. Last year it was some history person, this year it's this Vitruvious. Who knows what it will be next year? But that's kids for you. At least it's not dressing up in girls' clothes like my friend Ellie's boy. Six and wants to go to school in dresses." After half an hour, it was either end the call or poke a pencil through his own eye.

"Thank you so much for your help, Mrs Sully. I'm afraid I need to go now."

She was still talking as he hit the red button. He could tick one thing off his list. Kaylan had told him the truth about coming to Llanfair. Charlie doubted the veracity of anything else Kaylan had said.

CHARLIE MADE himself a drink before re-dialling the United States. In the bigger office, he could hear Eddy talking on the phone and pecking at his keyboard. He was tempted to see how Eddy was getting on with the fire bomber, then recognised it was another way to put off the inevitable. To his relief, both the Pepperdines were at home, though he realised after dialling that it was very early in the morning.

"Do you have news? Is Rico OK?" Mrs Pepperdine cried as he identified himself.

Charlie took a breath before answering and his hesitation was enough to set all the alarm bells ringing on the other side of the world.

"Is your husband with you, Mrs Pepperdine?" Charlie asked.

A deeper, male voice answered. "Michael Pepperdine here. You're on loudspeaker. Tell us what's happening."

As Charlie said the necessary words, he heard cries and sobs from Mrs Pepperdine, and Michael Pepperdine's carefully enunciated questions: "Are you sure that it's Rico? Can we see him? How did he die?" And again, "Are you sure?"

"We have a recent photograph of Rico, and the person"—Charlie was careful not to say *body*--"we found had a tattoo of a pine tree on his upper arm. We belive that it is Rico, but to be completely certain, we'd be grateful if you could access your son's dental records."

He heard "It's not him, see they aren't certain," in a high pitched, despairing voice that cut him like a knife.

Then the deeper voice. "That's not what he said, Brianna. Can we see our son, detective?" Michael Pepperdine asked.

"Of course, though you may prefer to remember him as he was." Charlie said, hoping that they would change their minds. The body he had seen was not a fit sight for grieving parents. "You'll need to make arrangements to get to Wrexham in north Wales. We can help with that." Charlie paused for a swallow of coffee and another deep breath before the next question from Michael Pepperdine.

"Why is a detective calling? What happened to Rico?"

"We don't know," Charlie said, honestly. "There are suspicious circumstances, and as you know, your son had been missing for a week. There will be a post-mortem examination which should tell us more."

"*I knew we should never have let him go! I want my baby …*"

Charlie heard the voice of Rico's mother in the background, and the sound of something smashing, probably crockery. He didn't have long, and there were things he needed to know.

"I do have a couple of questions, Mr Pepperdine. I know this isn't a good time, but it would be extremely helpful."

"Ask."

"Thank you, sir. My main question is this: do you know why Rico chose to do his degree here in Llanfair?"

Charlie heard a deep and troubled sigh.

"My son wanted to study painting in Europe. He isn't the most academic person, and his grades aren't great, actually, they're awful. I'll be honest, I don't know whether he's a good painter or not. I just know that it's all he ever wanted to do." There was another sigh. "He applied to places in France and Italy, and in London, but they wouldn't even look at his work because his basic education was so poor. The truth is, he can barely read and write. Why that mattered when all he wanted was to paint, I don't know. But apparently it does." Silence fell. Even Mrs Pepperdine's sobbing had stopped. Charlie could still hear Eddy in the outer office, and the occasional car on the road outside.

"I may as well tell you. It doesn't matter now. He applied to Llanfair along with all the others, and they turned him down, just like all the others. Then we got a call from one of the professors. He said that Rico was very talented, and they'd love to have him, but there were strict academic standards set down by your government. But there might be a way around it. *A donation to college funds* is what he called it. Fifty-thousand dollars. I paid it, because that's what my boy wanted …" Charlie heard the sound of sobbing and then, "I have to go," and the call ended.

15

Family Love

Charlie hadn't meant to cry. Crying wasn't something he did. He didn't realise he was crying until the first teardrop fell wetly onto the desk in front of him. As for why he was crying, he was crying for the Pepperdines who would pay a huge bribe to get their son a college place, and Mrs Sully, who would forgive Kaylan for anything, because that's what parents did. And for himself, a little, because his parents wouldn't forgive him anything. But mainly for the Pepperdines, whose son wouldn't be going home, and whose hearts were breaking. He put his arms on the desk and let the tears come, but only for a minute because he had work to do.

He didn't hear the office door open, or Eddy's footsteps. He felt himself gathered into a pair of strong arms, and heard Eddy's soft breath in his ear, whispering comforting nothings. Charlie leaned into Eddy's body and felt some of the tension ease. The next thing he knew, Eddy was lifting Charlie's head from the desk, and stroking his damp cheeks, with big, strong thumbs.

"Come here," Eddy said, not giving Charlie much choice. And then his lips were on Charlie's, warm, and tasting of coffee and a little of tears. His body responded, and Eddy felt the response, sliding his hands though Charlie's hair, and then, slowly, down Charlie's back and around his arse, pulling him closer. Charlie opened his lips, letting Eddy's tongue in to tangle with his own, and it was delicious. Eddy groaned quietly. Charlie's dick was getting in on the act and was telling him that *this* would give him a break from the constant anxiety, *this* would harm no one, *this* would help him to focus.

Then sense returned.

Charlie wriggled out of Eddy's arms, putting as much distance as he could between the two of them in the tiny office.

"Um, not what I want," Charlie said feeling the blush rising up his neck and spreading across his cheeks. "We're at work."

"Felt exactly like what you wanted," Eddy said, "and we won't always be at work."

"You took me by surprise. Sorry." Charlie didn't know where to put himself, or what to do with his limbs. He had kissed Eddy back and pressed his groin into Eddy's huge thigh. Not objected to Eddy's hands on his arse. But Eddy was not who he wanted, even if they hadn't been at work. He was suddenly afraid that he'd been giving out the wrong signals. Singing along to George Ezra in the car and including Eddy in his decision-making. Only, he didn't think he had. He'd treated Eddy as a colleague, though he had wondered about Eddy getting into his personal space a couple of times. *Oh, what the hell.* He just needed to be clear, right now.

"You'll come round, and it'll be fun, you and me," Eddy said neutrally, no sneering in his voice, simply a quiet confidence. Charlie knew at that moment that he wouldn't, ever. That Eddy was a potentially good colleague, a nice looking and sexy man, but Charlie had spent his entire childhood being told what he ought to do, by people who were certain that they knew better than him. His first instinct was to assume that Eddy was right, that he would come round and have fun, but he was learning that instinct, unchecked, often led to misery.

Instead, Charlie held on to DCI Ravensbourne's comment that he had done well and her confidence that he knew what he was doing. He thought of Mal Kent's trust in him, and of the way he, Charlie, had persuaded Tom to see things differently.

"Not going to happen," he said, but smiled to take the sting from his words. "Tell me about white van man."

"I'll tell Ravensbourne, when she comes over," Eddy said and left the room.

Charlie followed. "You can tell me, now," he said, without aggression.

For a moment, it looked as if Eddy would refuse. The air in the bigger room was cold and still, smelling faintly of damp and the PVC coating on the hi-vis jackets hanging in a line on the wall. There was little light coming through the tiny window from the grey sky outside. The fluorescent tube buzzed quietly above their heads.

"The gardener's lad, Gwilym Bowen knew where the keys were to the van, and where the petrol was stored, and when the owner was going out. He fits the description perfectly. He's also Harrington-Bowen's nephew. The bad news is that he's disappeared. He doesn't have an address, just dosses down at friends."

"You think Harrington-Bowen sent him? Or could he have another motive?" Charlie asked. "Anything helpful on that?"

Eddy shook his head. "Nothing. It's not as if we could ask old H-B if he sent his nephew to firebomb the station. Well, we could, but I doubt he'd admit it. Nope. We have to find young Gwilym, and how we're supposed to do that with everything else going on, is above my pay grade."

"Did you find anything interesting about Harrington-Bowen?" Charlie asked.

"He's on his third divorce, and he's either 'one of the

best', or an unpleasant time-server who can't keep his dick in his pants, and is probably living beyond his means. It depends who you ask, and whether they're a member of the funny-handshake brigade."

"With the Masonic contingent finding him to be 'one of the best' I suppose."

"Got it in one, Sarge."

"Better get started looking for Gwilym then. Friends, family, mobile number," Charlie said. "Give you something to do until the next disaster strikes."

DCI RAVENSBOURNE WAS SITTING at the conference table in Tom's office, drinking tea from a porcelain mug, biscuit crumbs scattered on her lap, when Charlie arrived at the college to take up Tom's offer of a look at the staff files. Tom, Charlie thought, was beginning to look as if he belonged in the beautiful office. He'd clearly seen through Ravensbourne's startling appearance to the sharp detective underneath. The secretary, Ann, showed him in, apparently not sure whether he'd come to report to Tom or the DCI. Faced with both of them, Charlie wasn't sure either. But he accepted the seat he was offered, and a mug of tea, and looked hungrily at the few biscuits left on the plate. He hadn't eaten since breakfast and it felt like a long time ago. His stomach rumbled loudly.

"Sorry," he said, and it happened again.

Tom stood up and went to the door. "Ann, do we have any sandwiches or sausage rolls or something to feed a starving police officer?"

"I'll be fine," Charlie mumbled, red with embarrassment.

"You'll be even finer with something to eat," Ravensbourne said. Charlie smiled, though in truth he still found her disconcerting.

"I spoke to the parents of both Kaylan and Rico," Charlie said. "There are some things I need to check, and then I want to look at the files, as we discussed." Ravensbourne looked sideways at Charlie. "Those things concern the college, ma-- boss, so I thought I could ask Tom about them straight away."

Ravensbourne raised her eyebrows at Charlie's use of Tom's given name, but said nothing. The secretary knocked on the door and opened it, bringing a plate of neatly cut triangular sandwiches and a slice of chocolate cake. Charlie's stomach growled again.

"Eat something, so we can hear ourselves think," Ravensbourne commanded. Tom caught Charlie's eye, and winked. Charlie ate two triangles as quickly as he could, trying not to drop crumbs. Then he took a swallow of tea and recounted what he'd learned from Mrs Sully and the Pepperdines.

"Mrs Sully said that she didn't think Kaylan was very good at art, and the family expected him to follow his father into computers. But he came here. I'll be honest, Mrs Sully did go off on a few tangents, but I'd still be interested to find out whether Kaylan is the kind of talented student you want to attract. There doesn't seem to be any doubt that he's keen, but is he any good?"

Tom leaned forward, hands crossed on the table. "I could look at his application, though, as you know, I'm a printmaker, not a painter. But we ask to see their sketchbooks as well as finished works. It's all on the computer. There should be a transcript of his grades from his high school and a letter from his teachers."

"The thing is," Charlie went on, "Mr Pepperdine said that Rico was barely literate, but was desperate to study art in Europe. No one wanted him, because of his difficulties, including this place. But then the Pepperdines got a call out of the blue saying he *could* come here, in exchange for fifty-thousand dollars. The Pepperdines paid up, and here he is, or was."

"Fifty-thousand dollars? On top of the fees and living costs?" Tom's voice had risen by at least an octave.

"Donation to college funds," Charlie said. "I was wondering whether Kaylan, who pays his own way to spite his parents, might also be making a donation. And whether there are any other students contributing above and beyond the standard fees."

Tom had his head in his hands, shaking it from side to side.

"It could be legitimate," Ravensbourne said.

"It *could be*," Tom replied. "But then I've been here pretty continuously since I did my PhD, and I have never heard of such donations. We need them, sure. We're always short of money. Making art is much more expensive than you think. Keeping up this bloody building costs a fortune. Every year some developer or other comes to beg us to sell it, but no, we carry on." He looked out of the huge window at the courtyard beyond. A few students were standing around talking, despite the grey skies. The fountain played. The piles of leaves were scattering themselves ready to be swept up again the next day.

"The only reason, *the only reason*, we keep going is that we attract enough international students, paying eye-watering fees, to balance the books. And the only reason we can do that is because we have the reputation of it being bloody hard to get a place. Letting sub-standard students in, even for fifty grand each, undermines the whole financial structure." Tom shook his head again, and pushed his hair back behind his ears.

"Easy enough to find out," Ravensbourne said. "You must have a finance office. Just ask them."

Tom's face cleared. He stroked his beard, put his hair behind his ears and reached for the phone. When it was answered, Tom said, "David, Tom Pennant. I wonder if you could pop along to my office for a moment. Something rather odd has come up."

Charlie thought Tom made a convincing college principal, and wondered what his colleagues would think if they had seen him in the Rainbow Club with his sleeves rolled up, drinking rum. Then he remembered the wife and children.

David, when he arrived, was a thin, harried-looking man with a comb-over and an elderly suit. Tom made quick introductions. Charlie enjoyed David's look of surprise at the contrast between Ravensbourne's rank and her appearance.

"There is a suggestion," Tom said, passive voice all the way, "that the college is in receipt of funds from some international students, extra to the fees and living costs. Voluntary donations. Possibly in exchange for, shall we say, a relaxation of admission criteria."

David had looked harried before. Now he looked as if the demons were gripping his ankles to begin pulling him into the fiery pit.

"That would be quite wrong, Principal. Against all college policies," he said.

"I know that, David," Tom enunciated with great care, spitting the words out between clenched teeth. "My question is whether it happened."

16

Fiery pit

TUESDAY 4.30PM

David scurried off, as if pursued by the hounds of hell, expressing complete certainty that no such donations had been made, but promising to check anyway. Immediately. Charlie took the opportunity to eat the rest of the sandwiches, and to consider whether he could manage the cake, before Tom asked the obvious next question.

"Who did the Pepperdines say called them to ask for money?"

"Mr Pepperdine couldn't remember. I don't know if he genuinely couldn't remember, or if it was the shock of learning that Rico was dead. He did say that he got an official Llanfair College of Art invoice, and bank details, and that's how he paid. But Mrs Sully, Kaylan's mother said that Kaylan was in touch with Vitruvious before he came here, more than once. So that's where I wanted to start. With his file."

Ravensbourne's phone rang. Either she had a strange sense of humour, or a wicked grandchild, but the ringtone was the B52s singing *Love Shack*. She looked at the phone and excused herself. Tom and Charlie grinned at each other, then Charlie remembered the wife and children *again*, and asked to see Vitruvious's file.

"Hang on," Tom said. He got a sheet of A4 out of his desk drawer and waved it at Charlie. "I got Ann to make me this crib sheet on how to get into the personnel files. I haven't looked at them before. Eat the cake, this'll take me a couple of minutes."

Charlie ate the cake. It was on the dry side but still very welcome.

"This is weird," Tom said. "Let me start again." He began following the steps on his crib sheet, ticking them off with a pencil as he went. "Right, Vitruvious, enter …" He turned the laptop to face Charlie. "No file of that name exists," read the text in the little box. "Please check and try again."

"That was the third time," Tom said. "The system is working. I've found my own file." He turned the laptop back to face himself and clicked a few times before turning it back. "It's even up to date."

The screen had multiple boxes with text. The first one read: "Pennant, Tomos Dylan, Principal (Acting)."

"Tomos Dylan?" Charlie asked. "Really?"

"Do not go there. My father's idea of a joke. I simply wanted you to see that it works. I've tried a couple of others, and they're fine too. Only Vitruvious is missing. Let me ask Ann." Tom went next door to the secretary's office.

Charlie walked round the room, looking out of the window onto the courtyard and over the rooftops to the hills beyond. Then he examined the bookcases. There were a lot of glossy exhibition catalogues, thick and heavy with shiny covers and the sheen of expensive colour printing on each page. Most had their spines facing towards the room, but a few showed the front cover, and one of these caught his eye. He picked it up and carried it to the table: *Habitatons: Tomos Pennant.*

The image on the front cover was of a block of flats too tall for the page. The building itself was drawn in delicate black lines. Some of the windows were empty. Others contained tiny tableaux of ordinary life. There were families eating, single people watching TV, someone playing with a dog, two children fighting, lovers kissing. Each of the tableaux was coloured, but delicately. Charlie opened the book. A double page spread showed the same house on each page—a simple semi-detached house of which there must be millions in the UK. On the left, the outside of the house was rendered in the same delicate lines, an image of something mundane made beautiful. On the opposite page, the building was opened up like a dolls' house, so that every room could be seen in all its detail. Inky colours glowed, trapped between delicate lines of drawing. On the next page was a thatched cottage, looking like a picture postcard, except for a single window through which a man could be seen sitting alone, drinking whisky. A book had fallen to the floor beside his chair, and there was a cat peering around a door in the back of the room. When Charlie saw the cat, he exclaimed, touching the image with his finger, as if to stroke its fur.

A voice came from close behind him. "Not the fucking cat. Please tell me you're not looking at the cat." Charlie looked up at Tom who was grimacing. "My daughter Ziggy asked for that cat, and fair play, it will pay her university fees with enough left over for her sister. But am I to go down in history as the man who drew a cat in a thatched cottage? Wallpaper, like Vitruvious says. Look." Tom took the book and turned several pages. This time the images were of static caravans in rows, like the huge holiday parks on the coast. Some were empty, others had coloured images through the windows. Ordinary people, doing ordinary things. Charlie found it moving, in a way the cat hadn't moved him. The cat was cute; these made him see the world differently.

"I don't know what to say," Charlie said. "I've never seen anything like them. I'm a bit stunned to be honest. Is this what you were doing in New York?"

"Some of it, some other things too. Drawing mostly. The

prints would have come later. I'd be happy to show you. I could make dinner--he winked--"and then I could show you my etchings. Go on, I'd love to."

Charlie thought that he would love to as well. Except that Tom had a family and even if he hadn't, from what he had seen on the pages of the book, Tom was so far out of his league Charlie would need a rocket to get close. Anyway, there were crimes to deal with.

"Could your secretary find Vitruvious's file," he asked, his tone carefully neutral.

Tom's brightness faded. "No," he said.

Charlie didn't know whether it was his own refusal to acknowledge Tom's offer of dinner and etchings, or the missing Vitruvious file, but the big man slumped down into his chair, his shoulders hunched and his chin dropping towards his chest. The catalogue closed itself on the table in front of Charlie. Charlie noticed that the gallery where the exhibition had been held was one even he had heard of.

It was a shame, but there it was. He would love to talk more with Tom about the images, but there was no point in wishing for things that couldn't happen. Charlie thought Tom looked sad, and had the urge to make it better. Whether he would have indulged the urge, he didn't find out. The door opened to Ravensbourne. Molecules of fresh cigarette smoke entered the room first, followed by the untidy figure busily tucking her phone back into her trouser pocket.

"That was Hector Powell," she said. "He's the pathologist, does post-mortems. He's very good," she added to Tom. "We got lucky and he did the PM as soon as they got the body back. The victim didn't die where we found him. Also no surprise that he'd been dead for between three and four days. As for what killed him, Hector was less sure. But he said that he's going to test for every drug under the sun. The thing he wanted us to know was that the victim hadn't eaten anything for several days before he died, and that the body showed signs of severe dehydration. It's entirely possible that the dehydration was the cause of death."

"Kaylan was dehydrated," Charlie said. "He needed a day in hospital on an intravenous drip to recover. Is dehydration associated with memory loss?"

"Exactly what I asked Hector," Ravensbourne said. "He said not, and that's why he was testing for drugs like Rohypnol —which do cause memory loss."

"We need to talk to Kaylan again," Charlie said. "About this, and about whether he paid for his place here. Not that he's been willing to tell us much, so far."

"Can I help?" Tom's voice was unexpected. "I could look at his application if you like, see if I think it would meet our admission criteria. I could look at both of them, Kaylan and Rico."

Ravensbourne nodded. "Please," she said. Tom went back to his laptop.

"I know how to access those records—we all have to evaluate a bunch of them every week. There's no off-season when it comes to applying for a place here." He clicked about with much more confidence than he had shown when looking for staff records, but after a while, the pace of his keystrokes slowed, and then stopped. He went back to the keyboard and clicked some more. Charlie sidled over, looking at as much of the screen as he could see. His best guess was that he was looking at a series of photographs of ceramic sculptures. Tom snatched up the desk phone.

"Peter, Tom Pennant," he snapped, visibly irritated. "Why do I not have access to the admissions files for painting students?"

They all heard the reply. "You do have access. To all the admissions files."

"Excellent. So perhaps you would like to come up here and demonstrate that. Because what I have on my screen is an irritating pop-up telling me that access is denied."

There was silence from the other end, and then, "I don't know what the problem is, Tom. I can't get access either. I'll get back to you as soon as."

Charlie's phone buzzed. Eddy.

"Sorry to bother you, sarge, but my computer has died. I tried the others, and they died too. So I'm going to use the one in your office if that's OK?"

"Well, yes, but hang on, what do you mean, all the computers have died?" Charlie asked. Because this was yet another kind of sabotage. Maybe not as dramatic as setting fire to a car, but it was the unseen enemy once more.

He heard Eddy's breathing, as if he had more to say. He did.

"I was getting some weird messages. They just appeared in the corner of the screen."

"And?" Charlie said.

"And if I ignored them, they went away after a minute or so. But they were irritating as hell, so I closed one rather than wait for it to go. Which is when the computer died."

"OK." Charlie said, "I'll bite. What are they, these weird messages?"

"No easy way to say it, but they're all about you. About that court case in Spain. Newspaper headlines. Bits of the evidence. Pictures of you. Things you said."

"Tom had one earlier," Charlie said. "They were on the other computers too? So Patsy and Mags will have seen them?"

"I guess," Eddy said.

Charlie would have to resign. There was no way past this.

"What's wrong?" Tom asked.

Charlie shook his head. What could he say? I made a mistake, picked up the wrong bloke on holiday, and someone is using it to disrupt the investigation. The bleakness he felt must have shown on his face, because the next thing he was breathing in stale cigarette smoke and his arm was being clutched, strong fingers digging into his bicep. Ravensbourne grasped Charlie's phone.

"Edwards," she snapped, "what?"

"Something odd with the computers, boss."

"Eddy…"

Eddy told her. Without comment she ended the call and gave Charlie his phone back.

"Right," she said, shaking Charlie's arm. "The entire bloody country knows you shagged the wrong bloke. I don't care, Pennant here keeps giving you googly eyes so I don't think he cares, and if Eddy cares he can talk to me about it. So you can either go to pieces or get on with the job, and we don't have time for you to go to pieces."

"No, boss," Charlie said, hoping that was the right answer, or should it have been "Yes, boss?"

"Charlie!" Ravensbourne said, bringing his focus back into the room.

"Computers, boss. Mags or Patsy, I don't remember which said that Harrington-Bowen's sergeant used to send pop-up dick pics to the women in the station. Jared Brody. Could it be him? Disrupting all the computers? Is that even possible?"

There was a gentle knock at the door. Ann poked her head round. "David from Finance is here," she said.

Tom nodded, and the emaciated Finance Director entered.

"Let me guess," Tom said, "your computer system denies you access to the information you need?"

David looked puzzled. "No, Principal. I came to tell you that there are no records of any additional donations to college funds of the kind you suggested."

17

Thanks, but no thanks
TUESDAY 5PM

The luxurious office fell silent when David left. Ann was still in the doorway, and she came to attention first.

"More coffee, I think," she said.

"I'm ready for gin," Tom said. "But I don't think there is any."

Ann raised her eyebrows but left, presumably to make the coffee.

Ravensbourne sat back down at the conference table, pushing the catalogue to one side. She looked at Tom. "I still want to know if Rico and Kaylan, and maybe others, got places here when they shouldn't. In the absence of their application records, can you find out?"

Tom nodded slowly. "I can ask their tutors if they were any good, I suppose."

"Why don't you do that, and ring Charlie when you find out. Ideally very soon. Charlie and I need to go."

Charlie felt his arm grabbed again, and followed Ravensbourne out of the office and then out of the college into the street. The shops were still open, although Charlie noticed that the bakery shelves were almost empty, and the butcher next door was washing his counters. There were a few people about, some looking in shop windows, others standing around chatting, and others marching along with their heads down as if on some kind of urgent errand. The skies were clear, though the sun was going down, and the breeze had strengthened, stirring up the fallen leaves and adding to their number. People were wrapping their coats more tightly around themselves, Charlie included. He wondered if he should have ordered a scarf as well as the coat.

Ravensbourne ducked into the doorway of a closed takeaway chicken shop to shelter from the wind and light a cigarette. Then she pointed to the bench beside the war memorial, and the two of them walked over to it and sat down. An empty crisp packet blew onto Ravensbourne's shoe. She picked it up and handed it to Charlie, so he could put it in the bin a couple of yards away. When he sat down again, the cigarette was finished, and Ravensbourne had her little notebook out.

"The question is," she said, "how many separate cases are we dealing with here? Is Rico's death in any way connected to the assaults on women students? And is any of it connected to the attack on the police station, weird messages on computers and possible financial fraud at the college? Charlie?"

"My instincts say they must be," Charlie said. "Because this is a very small town, and even though the college is a big deal, we're still not talking about that many people. The previous college principal and the Llanfair police colluded to cover up the assaults. The college and the police are connected. But how it all ties together, I don't know. I don't know how the fraud comes in, or if that's something separate. Except it seems to involve the same people: Vitruvious, Rico, Kaylan. Sorry, boss, thinking aloud."

Ravensbourne made some marks in her book.

"Do you trust those two police women? Jellicoe and Hargreaves?"

Charlie thought, and had no hesitation in answering. "Yes,

boss. Patsy Hargreaves was the original whistleblower, and Mags Jellicoe helped her compile the information. You've had them asking questions around the college all day, so you trust them. So, a definite yes."

"Good. I agree. What are you going to do next?" Ravensbourne asked.

Charlie felt the first spike of panic since Ravensbourne had arrived. *You tell me, you're the SIO.*

But Ravensbourne lit another cigarette and said nothing. Charlie focussed on slowing his breathing. Everything Ravensbourne said suggested that she thought his answer would be worth listening to.

"Um, re-interview Kaylan. He's the key, I think, though I'm not sure he will co-operate. Keep looking for Gwilym. Find out what we can about Vitruvious, and interview him. I think he's avoiding us. Talk to the Pepperdines again to see if they have the records of the payments they made, because fifty-thousand dollars is a lot of money, and if there were more payments like that… Get a forensic accountant to look at the college books. Catch up with any witnesses to Rico's body being moved. See if we can work out why it was left where it was. Was it supposed to make a statement? Or was it just a convenient spot?"

"And Harrington-Bowen and his cronies?"

"I hope, boss, that if we can get the answer to some of the other questions, a bright light will shine on Harrington-Bowen and Jared Brody …" Charlie trailed off. "Someone, or several someones, are trying to disrupt every part of the investigation, and stop us being able to focus. I'm guessing they think they can get their jobs back, and if we haven't found anything by the time they're back in charge, the secrets will stay buried for ever. So they are trying to keep us chasing our tails until then. We have to ignore the distractions."

Ravensbourne smiled and slapped Charlie's thigh so hard that the sound made a couple of passers-by look up in surprise. He thought that the longer he spent with Ravensbourne, the more bruises he would accumulate.

"Good. Ring me tonight with an update." She pulled out her phone and told whoever answered to pick her up by the war memorial as soon as they could. "Might just have time for another ciggy," she said.

Charlie stood up as if on automatic pilot. She was going to go, and he'd be on his own again. Except he had a plan, his plan, and Ravensbourne had, in her own peculiar way, signed off on it. His legs began to move in the direction of the police station, his mind racing, trying to put the tasks into some kind of logical order. *We'll start with a whiteboard.*

HE AND EDDY found a whiteboard behind the row of hi-vis jackets, and set it up in the break room, leaning up against some chairs. They found a set of coloured markers in a desk drawer and Charlie wrote the names of the people they were interested in across the top:

Kaylan Sully
Inigo Vitruvious
Gwilym Bowen
Nigel Harrington-Bowen
Jared Brody
Rico Pepperdine (dec)

DOWN THE SIDE, he wrote the items needing investigation:

Rico's death
Moving Rico's body
Kaylan's missing week
Arson attack on cars
Computer disruption at college
Computer disruption at police station
Alleged payments for college places

Assault(s) on female student(s)
Videos in H-B's desk
Patsy and Mags being followed

EDDY MADE them both a drink and they sat and stared at the board. Charlie drew a line between Gwilym and Harrington-Bowen, adding the word *nephew* and connecting Gwilym to the arson attack. "We don't know it was him," Charlie said. "But he fits the description, he's connected to someone we *know* doesn't want us to succeed, and he's disappeared. We need to find him."

Eddy nodded. "I've been making a list of all his mates, and his family, and I've got his mobile number, so we can ask for that to be tracked. We can get round most of his family and friends in one evening. Small town." Charlie shook his head.

"Phone track first. We haven't got the resources to spend looking anywhere he might not be. If you see what I mean."

Eddy grinned. "I'll ring Wrexham as soon as we're done."

They stared at the board some more.

"Why Vitruvious?" Eddy asked. "I can't say I took to him, but why him, out of all the tutors?"

"Vitruvious is the senior painting tutor. We know he was in contact with Kaylan over the summer. Rico was a painting student. The painting students' applications have disappeared. Vitruvious wasn't where he was supposed to be when Patsy and Mags went to find him. There's something there."

"There's no connection to Harrison-Bowen or Gwilym," Eddy said.

"No connection that we've found," Charlie replied.

Noise from the corridor announced the return of Patsy and Mags, both complaining of the cold wind and asking for cups of tea. Charlie obliged while the two women studied the board.

"Don't suppose you stopped at the shop on your way back?" Eddy said.

"Didn't need to," Patsy replied and opened the fridge. "Cupcakes, anyone?"

Charlie almost groaned. He had a passion for the ridiculously over sugared cakes, and the more outrageous the decoration, the more he liked them. He made a grab for a lemon-drizzle confection.

"What's *college computer disruption* and *fraud?*" Mags asked.

Charlie explained. He added, "Tom, the acting principal, has been getting those pop-ups about me, the same as you have been getting here." Mags blushed furiously, but Patsy just looked interested.

"We didn't want to tell you," Mags said.

"I've had my name in every paper in Britain," Charlie said.

"She means that she thinks you're a good bloke and she didn't want you to be upset," Patsy said. Eddy snorted.

"Thanks, I think," Charlie said.

Mags blushed even harder, and wrapped her arms below her breasts. "Patsy," she snapped, voice higher than usual. "You aren't talking to idiots. Please try a little respect, or even common courtesy."

Patsy opened her mouth to say something. Mags held a finger to her own lips and glared at Patsy.

"Right," Patsy said.

Time to move on, Charlie thought.

"Did you find anyone who saw Rico's body being moved?" he asked.

"Nope," said Patsy, hastily swallowing a mouthful of cake. "The front entrance to the workshop is only overlooked by a couple of windows in the main building. There is a back entrance, and the scenes of crime people think the lock might have been picked. Or not. It's only a wooden door and the lock is ancient. The key was hanging up inside, so it could also have been borrowed and copied." She stopped to take a swallow of tea, and Mags took up the story.

"Anyway, the point is that there's loads of room to get a van, or a small truck, right up to the back door and they, whoever they are, could have unloaded without anyone seeing anything. Violet — the woman who uses the workshop — has a van she uses to collect her… materials, and that's how she brings them. A white Ford Transit."

"When was she last there?" Charlie asked.

"Not since the middle of last week. Her father was ill, so she took a couple of days off." Mags said. "He's fine," she added, as if they might be interested. Charlie was too busy thinking about the white Ford Transit crashed into the front of his car, in the yard behind the police station. Surely that would be a coincidence too far?

"No one would be surprised to see a white van being unloaded at the back of the workshop then?" he asked. "But did anyone see it while Violet was away?"

"One of the campus services officers thought he might have done, last night. But he couldn't be sure. He said it might have been another day. But it's all we've got."

Charlie added "white Ford Transit van" and "Monday night?" to the whiteboard.

"Are we sure it wasn't Violet's own van last night?" Eddy asked.

Mags shook her head. "No, it's the only vehicle she has. She used it to get to her Dad's."

"Where's that?" Eddy said.

Patsy looked at her phone. "Somewhere called Denholm. It's in Lancashire."

Eddy began fiddling with his phone and held his hand up. "Denholm is less than five miles from Brocklehurst. Brocklehurst, ladies and gents, is where Kaylan Sully walked into the local police station, claiming to have lost his memory." Eddy leaned back in his chair. "Fill your chart in, Sarge, we have a contender!"

Charlie added Violet's name to the whiteboard, along with the words "Denholm, Brocklehurst, and white Transit van. He drew a line to Rico's body.

"We have a possible connection," he said. "But that's all we've got. And it's not like we haven't got any others. I've met Violet. She's not tiny, but she's not big either. Shifting a dead body is hard work. I can't believe she could have done it by herself. But we need to talk to her, and have the van looked at for signs of the body. I want to know who else in this town has a white Ford Transit."

"We can't ignore the Brocklehurst thing, Sarge," Eddy said.

"I'm not ignoring it," Charlie said. "I'm not ignoring it so much that I think you should go and visit Violet's dad, and see if there's anywhere Rico and Kaylan could have been hidden. See if anyone else on our list has a Brocklehurst connection. Find out if anyone could have borrowed Violet's van. Bring the van in, get it looked at and ask the scenes of crime crew if there's anything in the workshop that could have been used to transport the body."

Eddy made notes. "Will do, Sarge. But we only have one working computer, and that's in your office."

"You don't need a computer to visit Violet's dad," Charlie said. "You should all know that we don't have much time. Ravensbourne made it clear that Harrington-Bowen and co. are itching to get back in here, and they've got a lot of friends. She didn't give me a limit, but I'd say we're already on borrowed time. I'd like us to do the interviews with Kaylan and the visit to Violet's dad this evening, because the clock is ticking."

"Just us four against the forces of evil, then," Eddy said.

Patsy giggled and Mags looked scared. Charlie thought that if it all went pear-shaped, Eddy would be re-absorbed back into Ravensbourne's team in Wrexham, and Patsy seemed to have an infinite capacity for doing the right thing and taking the consequences. He thought Mal Kent and Patsy probably had a lot in common. Mags worried him. She seemed the most fragile of the team, with emotions closer to the surface even than his own. Without her hi-vis jacket and equipment belt, she was curvaceous and softly rounded. Once again, she had only nibbled at half a cake, giving the rest to Eddy. He was no one to judge women, but he thought rather than try to lose weight, Mags should tell her cousin to buy her a bigger dress.

"Patsy and Mags. I want you to bring Kaylan in, and interview him formally. Try to get him to tell you where he was for the missing week, ask him if he knows Violet, or her workshop. Before you do, ask to see the paperwork to do with his admission—especially everything to do with money. How much are his fees, his accommodation, and how much of a donation did he give to the college. Find out if he was accepted into any other art colleges. Make it clear that he isn't being arrested, but it's a formal interview, under caution."

18

Predecessors
TUESDAY 6PM

Charlie should have asked Ravensbourne for another car. Llanfair was a small town, but Harrington-Bowen lived on the very outskirts. The sun was completing its descent behind the hills to the west of the town as he walked up a steep, narrow road lined with bungalows, all of which must have had magnificent views. It had been a long day, and showed no signs of ending anytime soon, and his legs ached at the effort of walking uphill. He passed a young man in a dark hoodie with some kind of pale logo who was almost jogging back down, and felt deep envy.

A couple of cul-de-sacs led off the road, with newer bungalows, until at the top of a rise, Charlie found the address he wanted. He was not surprised to find himself in front of a very large, newly built home, in a small close with three or four others. The windows were framed in fashionable dark grey with a matching front door, providing a pleasing contrast with the bright white render, and the green of the perfect lawn. A gleaming black Range Rover was parked outside on a gravel drive. Charlie made a bet with himself that when he rang the doorbell, a dog would bark, and it would be a cocker spaniel. He was right on both counts.

The dog was told firmly to go back to its basket, and Charlie looked at the man whose office he was occupying. Nigel Harrington-Bowen must have been very good-looking when he was younger, and despite his middle-aged spread he would probably still turn a few heads. His hair was thick, blond and shiny, his face lightly tanned and his eyes an attractive blue. He easily topped six feet, with broad shoulders and long legs clad in burgundy cord trousers and a black V-neck lambswool sweater. Charlie didn't need to look down to know that Harrington-Bowen's feet would be wearing loafers without socks.

"Inspector Harrington-Bowen? I'm DS Charlie Rees. We spoke on the phone. There are a few things I'd like your help with, sir, if you have a moment."

Harrington-Bowen's look of satisfaction was echoed by his expansive welcoming gestures. There was a generous porch with coat hooks and a shoe rack. The coats were the expected Barbours and duffels, but amongst the Hunter wellingtons was a grubby baseball cap with a V-shaped logo on the front. It didn't look like anything Harrington-Bowen would wear. Charlie was escorted along the wide hallway with its engineered oak floorboards, into a lounge painted in pale grey, with a deep grey carpet and deliberately mismatched sofas in green and blue velvet. An enormous television dominated one side of the room, and at the opposite end, an unlit wood burner stood in a recess lined with cut logs. French windows looked onto a small, well-manicured lawn. It could have been a show home, and maybe it had been.

"Sit down, DS Rees. I recognised you from your pictures, of course. Quite the media sensation. Perhaps not the fifteen minutes of fame you were hoping for." Harrington-Bowen laughed, and not in a pleasant way.

"No, sir," Charlie said, consciously arranging his face into an unthreatening neutrality. "I wanted to ask you about your nephew, Gwilym. Do you know where we might find him?"

Whatever Harrington-Bowen had expected, it wasn't this.

"Gwilym? Why are you asking me where he is?"

"We need to talk to him, so we're contacting his friends and relatives. He appears to be of no fixed abode." Charlie allowed his glance to encompass the perfectly appointed room as he spoke.

"You thought I might be keeping him here?"

"I don't know, sir. And you can't suggest where he might be found?"

"I believe I just answered that DS Rees."

Actually, you didn't. But let's move on.

"The other thing I wanted to ask you about were some videos we found in the police station, specifically on a data stick in your desk. These appear to be recordings of assaults on young women. I wondered what you can tell me about them."

"I would have thought that was more your sort of thing than mine, Rees." Harrrington-Bowen said with a sneer.

"The videos were in your office, sir, and since you mention it, no, they were not to my taste. I'm curious about whether you put them there. One of the videos appeared to show a very recent assault on a female student. You will understand we need to know where they came from."

The answer, like the appearance of the dog, was exactly as Charlie had expected: blustering denial. What Charlie couldn't determine was how far Harrington-Bowen was lying. Lying he certainly was. He asked all the wrong questions for someone who had never heard of such videos. But Charlie wasn't sure the inspector knew they were in his desk drawer.

"Who do you think could have put the material into your desk, sir?"

"How the hell should I know?" Harrington-Bowen snapped.

"It's very incriminating material, sir. I would think you would want to know where it came from." Charlie said.

"Obviously we will be sending it over to the technicians in Wrexham, to see if they can enhance the images. Maybe we can see who some of the people are, and where the events took place." Charlie had no idea if any of this was possible, but he guessed Harrington-Bowen didn't either.

Harrington-Bowen sprang to his feet. "What a ridiculous waste of police resources! Forensic examination of pornography." His face flushed. "Understand this, Rees, better men than you have tried to blackmail me, and failed. Get out of my house!"

Charlie left, without seeing the dog or hearing anything suggesting there was anyone else at home. But the baseball cap didn't fit, and Charlie couldn't imagine Harrington-Bowen covering his luxuriant hair with it. But collecting videos of young women being assaulted? That he could imagine with no difficulty at all. He set off back to the police station, turning the collar of his coat up against the chill.

As he walked, much easier on the way back, the baseball cap nagged at him. There was something about the logo. He'd seen it before, and recently. Suddenly, the V shape resolved itself into a pair of rabbit ears: the Playboy Bunny logo. The same logo that had been on the data stick in Harrington-Bowen's drawer. And, Charlie realised with a jolt, the same logo on the front of the hoodie worn by the young man he'd passed on the way up the hill. A young man he had noticed had a straggly beard. All of it like the witnesses' descriptions of the arsonist.

CHARLIE WAS out of breath by the time he got back to the station, full of news about his probable sighting of the arsonist and his connection to Harrington-Bowen. He found Patsy and Mags in despair.

"We cautioned Kaylan and it was water off a duck's back, "Mags told him.

"He's told you nothing?"

"Talks and talks until our heads are spinning, but not one bit of useful information has he shared. Lots of talk about how amazing Vitruvious is, lots of talk about how he's living in a police state. Lots of talk, full stop. He's an arrogant shit, and he's enjoying all the attention."

"Enjoying the attention?" Charlie asked.

"He's playing with us." Patsy said. "You got Eddy to look up anything that might have caused a week's lost memory, and there are both street and prescription drugs that would do it. But he'd have to have been given dose after dose, and he'd have been confused and delirious for a long time while they wore off."

"Anything about money?"

Patsy waved her hand airily. "Oh, my accountant deals with all that," she said in an appalling American accent.

"Right then, tell him he can stay in our luxury accommodations tonight and we'll see how he feels in the morning."

"We can't keep him here!" Mags exclaimed.

"It's a police station," Charlie said. "Therefore there are cells. Therefore we can keep him overnight."

"They're unusable," Mags said.

"Show me," Charlie replied. Because how bad could they be?

The answer was that the cells were horrible. For some reason, although the cell building was attached to one side of the police station, it had a separate entrance, like a granny annex on a private house. Charlie could imagine only that it had been added later, though why it hadn't been properly integrated, he didn't understand. Through the door was a short corridor with stairs to the upper floor at the end. To the right were the two cells. Each was an eight foot by six-foot grey concrete box, with a narrow concrete bench down one side. The doors were painted green, made of thick metal with a single peephole. At the far end of each, a stainless-steel toilet was bolted to the wall. The window was an eighteen-inch square of heavily barred glass. The whole lot stank of damp and black mould. Even if they cleaned the mould from the walls, it would still be freezing cold. There was electricity for lights, but no form of heating. Uninhabitable was an understatement.

Charlie sighed. They were going to have to send Kaylan back to his hall of residence and try again in the morning.

"Send the twerp home. He can walk. We know where to find him," Charlie told Mags.

"THAT'S THE OLD STAFF ACCOMMODATION?" Charlie asked, pointing to the stairs. Mags nodded, but Patsy was already halfway up.

"I've never been in here," she called over her shoulder. Charlie followed. The stairs were barely illuminated, though a doorway at the top was lit, with Patsy blocking it like a statue. Arriving behind her on a tiny landing, Charlie looked over her shoulder at what appeared to be a makeshift office. Patsy didn't move. She held her hands out to stop Charlie going into the room.

"Someone's been living here," she said.

He looked over her shoulder and could see the signs of recent occupation. A plug-in electric heater stood next to a cheap folding bed with a sleeping bag, pillows and a tangle of blankets. An open duffel bag spilled clothes onto the floor. A phone charging cable hung from another socket, next to a camping chair of dubious looking comfort. Takeaway containers and beer cans were about to overflow from a cardboard box obviously serving as a bin. The room smelled of stale beer, the remains of the takeaways, and underlying it all the sharp odour of petrol

"He must have spilled some petrol when he was making his firebomb," Patsy said, sniffing hard.

"Gwilym. Hiding right here under our noses," Charlie said. "No wonder we couldn't find him. Harrington-Bowen must have told him about the place."

Charlie thought about the big show home where Harrington-Bowen lived, and wondered how he could have allowed his nephew to squat in an almost derelict building.

Patsy grasped his arm. "Is that rats?" she said, pointing to the corner of the room where there was a doorway. Charlie could hear something, some kind of rustling, scratching noise. He hoped it wasn't rats, or if it was, they would stay where they were. He and Patsy stayed very still, listening. The air in the cold, damp, flat was silent, bar the noise of the occasional car on the road outside. The sounds started again, and Charlie knew what it was.

"Gwilym," he called, "we know you're in there. I can hear you sniffing. Come out and show yourself. Let's get you somewhere warm and talk about this."

There was no reply. Charlie pointed at Patsy and opened and closed his hand in a talking sign, then pointed at himself and made tiptoeing motions with his fingers. Patsy nodded.

"Gwilym," she called. "We've been looking for you. There's hot drinks and plenty of food downstairs. You must be freezing your nuts off up here. It's damp, and there are probably rats." She managed to keep up the talk as Charlie crept across the room to the doorway. He could hear the sniffing getting louder. With a shout, he threw the door open to reveal a tiny kitchen, as filthy as the rest of the flat, and Gwilym on the floor, his back pushed into the corner of the room, with an enormous knife held out in front of him, in a trembling hand. Tears and snot ran down his face and into his beard. He was shaking with cold. Charlie felt Patsy materialise beside him.

"Put the knife down, Gwilym," Charlie said. "We can't leave you here, and I don't want to have to call in armed police. So put the knife down."

Gwilym shook his head, and gripped the knife harder,

though he was still shivering. "Go away," he said in a watery voice.

"We can't do that Gwilym. You know that, don't you? Put the knife down and all this will be over."

"I'll kill myself," Gwilym said, voice high and trembling, body still shaking. "Don't come any closer, or I will."

"You've done nothing worth killing yourself over, really you haven't. We just want to talk to you, that's all." It was Charlie's turn to keep talking, keep Gwilym's attention on him as Patsy edged closer. He hoped to God she knew what she was doing.

"Killing yourself isn't as easy as it looks," Charlie said. "It hurts like hell, and there's lots of blood. Mostly it doesn't work. And do you want to die here, with all these spiders and in this cold? Come and have a cup of tea at least, downstairs in the warm. There are cakes too, if our colleagues haven't eaten them all. We could send for fish and chips. Do you like fish and chips?"

There was a sudden blur of movement, and the knife went flying across the room, slithering to a stop against a cupboard. Gwilym screamed and moved as if to go after it, but it was too late. Patsy had grabbed the hand that had held the knife, and Charlie was across the room in a single stride, handcuffs ready. As he clicked them into place, he felt Gwilym's freezing skin as his shivering intensified. Between the two of them, they helped Gwilym to his feet, his body obviously stiff from cowering in the corner for so long. He smelled of sweat and damp clothes, with a hint of petrol. They left the knife where it was, on the dirty floor. There would be time to collect it later.

19

Gwilym
TUESDAY 8PM

"What was *that?*" Charlie gasped as they led Gwilym down the stairs and out into the car park.

"Kickboxing," Patsy said. "I'm getting quite good at it, don't you think?"

"I hope I never annoy you," Charlie replied, and Patsy laughed.

The sky was clear enough to see the moon and a couple of the brightest stars, despite the street lamps. The earlier wind had dropped, along with the temperature. Charlie smelled woodsmoke hanging in the still air, and beyond it, the undefinable scent of a frost to come. Under his feet, a few charred spots showed where his car had stood. The foam had all gone, along with the van and the two cars. But he didn't need to worry about them tonight. He was certain he had the arsonist in handcuffs, and the knife suggested Gwilym might have other questions to answer. It was time to bring Ravensbourne up to date.

The Llanfair police station interview room was typical of the rest of the place. Small, dark and badly maintained. There was a faint smell of mould from the carpet, and there was no tape recorder or video camera, just a table bolted to the floor, and four chairs. But it was all they had. Feeling like he'd stepped back to the 1970s, Charlie handcuffed Gwilym to the table, and led Patsy and Mags to the break room next door. He rang Ravensbourne and put the phone on loudspeaker.

"Hi, Charlie," she said when she answered. "I'm glad you called. I was about to call you. I'm getting some grief about you harassing that Vitruvious bloke. Better leave him alone unless you have something solid. He seems to have a lot of media connections and he's threatening to use them."

"We haven't spoken to him, boss." Charlie said. The others all shook their heads in confirmation.

"Good. Keep it that way."

"I did arrest Gwilym Bowen though. He was hiding out in a kind of annex attached to the station. Ex-police flat, in really bad condition. He waved a big knife at us. The kind of knife the flasher uses. And, I'm pretty sure he's been at Harrington-Bowen's house. So I can arrest him for threatening us, even if he doesn't want to talk about anything else. But if we're keeping him overnight, it can't be here. There are cells, but you wouldn't keep an animal in them."

"I've heard. I'll send transport," Ravensbourne said. "He's yours until it arrives. Remember that Harrington-Bowen has plenty of friends in Clwyd Police." She ended the call.

If Charlie understood her correctly, Ravensbourne had given him until the transport arrived to get a confession out of Gwilym, because once he was moved to Wrexham, he'd be safely back under his uncle's protection. Fine.

"Let's make some tea and get on with it," he said to Mags and Patsy. "We've got about an hour to get Gwilym to tell us what he's been up to. Mags, go upstairs and get the knife from the kitchen and bag it up. Have a poke around and see if there's anything that suggests Molotov cocktail making." Mags left.

"Patsy, go and find a tape recorder, or a video recorder. There must be something we can use, to make it look more professional than just our phones." She left.

Charlie ran upstairs for a laptop and the data stick with the Playboy bunny logo. He took the laptop into the interview room and set it up. Patsy followed with the video recorder on a tripod. Gwilym's eyes widened as he watched them plug the equipment in to the one available socket, making a daisy chain of extension leads. There was a knock at the door. Charlie opened it to see Mags with a mug of tea and a sandwich on a plate.

"Gwilym," Charlie said. "Have a drink and something to eat. We need to ask you some questions."

Gwilym looked at the sandwich and shook his head. "Not hungry," he said. But he picked up the tea, wrapping his hands around the mug and hunching his body over it as if to warm himself.

"What questions?" Gwilym asked. He sounded nervous. "Are you going to tell my uncle?"

"Do you want us to?" Charlie asked.

Gwilym shook his head so hard that the tea began to slop over the side of the mug. "He'll be angry. He's angry enough with me already."

Doubt began to creep into Charlie's mind. Was Gwilym competent to answer questions? Mags would be the better person to have with him in the interview, he thought, so he asked her to stay. He told Gwilym his rights, double checked that he understood them, asked if Gwilym wanted a solicitor (he didn't) and made sure that the video recorder was picking everything up.

Then he produced the data stick from his pocket and plugged it into the laptop. The first of the videos began to play. A shadowy figure masturbating in front of a young woman; her face visible, tears rolling down her cheeks, arms wrapped around her body. Her sleeve had been cut, and the slash was easily visible. In the background, the video showed one of the cubicles in the art studios in the college building. It was dim, and the walls were out of focus, but Charlie could see grey and white paper pinned to the flimsy board walls. He stopped the video, and looked at Gwilym.

"I think that's you, Gwilym. It is you isn't it?"

Gwilym looked down at his mug of tea. "I never hurt them," he said, and the tap opened to a flood of words, all spoken into the cooling mug of tea. Gwilym confessed to all the assaults, remembering each of them in detail, describing how he waited until the college was quiet and then stalked the corridors, workshops and storage spaces for women on their own. "I cut their clothes. Only their clothes. I wanted them to know the knife was sharp. I wanted them to keep still and watch. But I wouldn't hurt them."

"The women didn't know that," Charlie said. Gwilym just repeated that he *wouldn't hurt them.*

"When did your uncle find out?" Charlie asked, because time was passing.

There was no answer.

"Your uncle," Charlie repeated.

"He caught me," Gwilym whispered into his mug. "In the college. I was watching a girl, and I heard him so I hid."

"What was your uncle doing in the college after everyone had gone home?"

"He was arguing about money with Mr Vitruvious. My uncle said Mr Vitruvious should give him more money, or he would have to sell the house. They were shouting at each other, and I must have made a noise because they stopped and my uncle found me. He asked me why I was there, and he … guessed. I think he might have guessed before." Gwilym's head was almost resting on the rim of the mug, his entire body curved into a donut around it. Suddenly, he looked up.

"What's going to happen to me?" he asked.

"Tonight you'll be going to Wrexham police station and in the morning you'll be asked about the things you've told us, by some other detectives. After that you'll probably be charged with the attacks on those women, and you'll go to court. If you are found guilty, then you'll go to jail."

Gwilym nodded. He pushed the mug away from him, across the table, and sat up straighter. Anger flashed in his eyes. "That's what my uncle said. He said he wouldn't let it happen as long as he was in charge, *because I never hurt them*. I shouldn't have to go to jail. But then you came."

"Is that why you set fire to my car?" Charlie asked.

"I shouldn't have to go to jail. I never hurt any of those girls. None of them." And that was the end of it. Every question got the same answer. Gwilym hadn't hurt anyone, and his uncle had told him he wouldn't be arrested or charged.

CHARLIE TOLD Mags to go home. She looked drawn and exhausted. She insisted that she was fine.

"Either you go willingly, or I make Patsy drive you," he said.

"I'm going," she said wearily.

"I'll walk you as far as the supermarket," Patsy said, "and if I can get some petty cash, I'll get a few supplies." She held her hand out and Charlie gave her two twenty pound notes. Then he rang Eddy, who said he'd be about fifteen minutes.

He was as good as his word, arriving at the same time as Patsy. He dived into the big bag-o-snacks even though Charlie was quite sure (from the faint odour of vinegar) that Eddy had already stopped for fish and chips. He helped himself to a Snickers bar, and dispatched it in a few bites. Charlie wordlessly handed him a cup of tea.

"So," he said, "is Violet still a contender?"

Eddy shook his head. "Her dad says she never left his side. It was touch and go whether he needed to go to hospital, which he didn't want. He had pneumonia, or the beginnings of it, and they gave him antibiotics. Thankfully for him, they worked. Apparently Violet goes to visit most weekends and sometimes a day in the week. I asked the neighbours. I asked the neighbours about the van, too. It never moved. Multiple witnesses prepared to swear it was outside the house all the time Violet was there." Eddy took a sip of his tea, found it cool enough to drink and swallowed half the cup. His suit looked as if it had spent the day scrunched up in a car, which it had, and Eddy's face showed the first signs of fatigue. He rubbed his hand over his face and through his cropped hair.

"I found something interesting though." He paused. Neither Charlie nor Patsy spoke. "Really interesting."

Patsy moved the bag-o-snacks out of Eddy's reach, and before he could react, tipped the rest of his tea in the sink.

"Hey!" He shouted. Patsy laughed.

"Stop milking it, tell us what you found, and I'll make you another cup. You found something interesting, Charlie arrested the flasher, and we found where he'd been living. Come on, big man, give."

Eddy's eyebrows almost reached his hairline. "The flasher?"

"Waiting for transport to Wrexham." Patsy said, and folded her arms with satisfaction. "In our interview room, such as it is."

Charlie sighed. "Eddy, mate, just tell us." Eddy winked at Patsy.

"You only had to ask," he said. He glanced over to Charlie, and lost the bantering tone. "I went in a couple of Violet's dad's neighbours' houses. Like I said, I was checking about the van. Anyway, three doors down, there's a Mr Volker. Elderly chap, dunno where he was from originally, but it wasn't

147

Lancashire. Inside, there are Llanfair College of Art posters all over the walls. Nicely framed. Exhibitions from students and staff. There was a big painting too, over the fireplace: a seascape. I didn't get much of a look at it, because Volker stood right in front. I asked about the van, and he said the same as everyone else, only he wasn't as pleasant about it. Then I asked about the posters and he goes all evasive, says he used to know someone who worked there. But some of the posters are recent — one from this summer. I tried to ask some more and he started talking about having to make a phone call and almost pushed me out the door."

"The obvious person to be bringing posters is Violet, surely?" Charlie asked.

"You would think so. Only Volker fell out with Violet's dad ages ago, and they haven't spoken for years. He told me the van was *cluttering the place up, taking up other people's spaces* and that it *was typical of that family.* By the end he was almost spitting. I didn't have time to ask anyone what the dispute was about. I came back. I mean, we can always ask Violet. My point is, someone apart from Violet has a connection to the area where Kaylan was found."

"Which would be a lot more useful if we knew for sure who it was," Patsy said. But she did make Eddy another cup of tea.

"Let's ask her now," Charlie said, and put the number into his phone. "DS Rees," he said when Violet answered. "My colleague spoke to your father today and I was wondering if you could tell me what is behind the dispute between him and his neighbour, Mr Volker?"

Charlie didn't know what he was expecting, but it wasn't laughter.

"The secret is out," Violet said, and laughed some more. "Sorry. Reinhard Volker is the father of our own senior painting tutor and class A poseur, Inigo Vitruvious. Only no one is supposed to know. Volker doesn't fit V's image. He's a refugee, but he's also a neo-Nazi, or as near as dammit. So right-wing that almost no one will speak to him, because they're all sick of being harangued about his latest conspiracy theory. V visits occasionally, but he doesn't stay long, and he hates anyone knowing. I'm assuming that's why he's so obsessed with his small boats stuff. I can't ask, because V doesn't speak to me, in case I betray his secret. It's pathetic."

Charlie listened to Violet and then watched as Eddy drew a line connecting Vitruvious with Kaylan's kidnap. When the call ended, they all looked at the whiteboard, with lines snaking all over connecting names and crimes. Charlie stood up, chose a red pen and circled Vitruvious's name.

"He's potentially connected to where Kaylan was found, and we know he had contact with Kaylan over the summer. He lives in an expensive village, and drives an expensive car. Is he living beyond his means? Is he the one requesting generous donations from sub-standard students?"

"Maybe," Eddy said, "but is there a connection between the generous donations business, and the disappearance of Kaylan and Rico? Because I can't see one."

Nor could Charlie, and by the look on her face, Patsy couldn't either.

They were all still staring at the board when the transport arrived for Gwilym, and once he'd gone, there was no need for any of them to stay. Charlie wiped a space on the board and wrote out a list of actions for the morning:

College Financial Records

Vitruvious finances/interview (why have we been told not to?)

Kaylan interview

Pepperdines — how did they pay?

Other painting students — did they pay extra? How?

Chase up forensics about white van(s)

Computer hacking? Jared Brody?

"That should keep us going for a bit," Eddy said, reaching

for the bag of snacks. Patsy was batting his hand away when her phone rang. She answered then almost fell into a chair.

"Oh my God, is she OK?" Patsy held the phone away from her face and turned to Charlie and Eddy, tears forming in her eyes. "Mags has been attacked by a man with a knife. She's pregnant and they're afraid she'll lose the baby."

20

Mags
TUESDAY 9.30PM

Nowhere in Llanfair was very far from anywhere else. Mags lived about ten minutes' walk from the police station: into the town, then past the college and out on the other side. For Mags, as for most of the townspeople, the college grounds were a regular cut-through. In the last few days, Charlie had seen how people simply turned in through the gates and walked across to cut off corners. Tom had told him that the library was open to anyone, and that the doctor's surgery for the whole town was on the campus itself. So, when Patsy said Mags had been attacked, Charlie assumed it had been at the college.

It almost was, but there was still police tape around the sheds and workshops at the back, and everywhere else was well lit. Students' Union people and campus services officers were walking round with big torches, unaware that the police had someone in custody. But the college was surrounded by a high wall which cast a deep shadow after dark. In the day, the outside of the wall was lined with cars; at night, most had gone. A few residents without private spaces parked there, but for the most part, it was empty. Except tonight, when there had been a man in a balaclava and black clothes, carrying a big knife.

Patsy's face was as white as a sheet. She kept saying, "OK, OK," to whoever she was listening to on the phone. When the call ended, she said, "That was Mags' husband. Mags has a knife wound on her arm, not too serious he says, but she got knocked over and the first responders are afraid of concussion and for the baby. The ambulance is on its way."

The three of them were on their feet, coats on, and out of the door by the time Patsy had finished speaking. They took the car, blue lights flashing, and arrived at the same time as the ambulance. Mr Mags stood holding his wife's hand, looking daggers at the three police officers. Their house was across the road and both he and some of the neighbours had heard Mags shouting and run out to help.

Mags turned to Charlie, blood dripping from her right hand. Her padded coat was torn, leaking its stuffing which was stained with blood. "It wasn't the flasher, I'm certain of it," she said. "Nothing like the man in the videos. This bloke was bigger and taller, a man, not a boy. I didn't realise that until I saw him tonight. Black clothes, but shoes, not trainers. A balaclava with just eye holes. Too dark to see the colour." A paramedic was speaking urgently about wanting to look at Mags' arm, and her husband kept saying, "She's pregnant. She was unconscious."

Mags pulled away. "I wasn't unconscious. I fell, that's all." She pointed to the ground in the darkest shadow under the wall. "My pepper spray. I didn't use it. I got it out of my pocket, and he knocked it out of my hand and swiped at me with the knife. If he touched it, there might be prints. I spat at him, so look at his clothes when you get him. I might have bled on him too." Mags gave an attempted smile.

"Which way did he go?" Charlie asked.

"Gate Street." Mags pointed to a narrow street on the other side of the road, with no pedestrians and few lights. The nearest end was blocked by bollards to stop cars. The attacker could have removed the balaclava and emerged into the better-lit streets looking like anyone else.

"Was he waiting for *you*, or just anyone?" Charlie asked, feeling the increase in tension emanating from Mags' husband and the paramedic.

"Mags, the baby," her husband said.

"The baby is fine," she said. "I'm fine, and I'm coming now." She turned her back on her husband to face Charlie. She wasn't fine, Charlie could see that, but he needed the answer to his question. "He was waiting for me, I think. I saw him standing in the shadow of the wall, and stepped out to walk past, and that's when he moved. We're right opposite our house. The whole wall is in shadow, but he chose to wait here."

"Mags," her husband said, and this time she listened.

"I'm coming," she said and allowed herself to be led to the waiting ambulance.

Even before it had closed its doors, Charlie had the big torch from the back of the police car, shining it down into the corner of the wall, where there was a pepper spray lying next to some dead leaves. "Bag it up," he said to Patsy, "and have a good look round in case there's anything else. Tape it off, so we can have another look in daylight. Eddy, Gate Street, look in the bins, gardens, anywhere he might have thrown the bala-clava or the knife. I'll speak to the witnesses."

Most of the neighbours had begun to drift back to their houses once the ambulance went on its way. He caught up with two of them as they crossed the road.

"DS Rees," he said. "Can I talk to you for a moment?"

In all, three sets of Mags' neighbours had heard her shouts, and run out of their houses. Everyone else in the small crowd of onlookers had been attracted by the blue flashing lights and commotion in a quiet street. The houses were close together, but semi-detached rather than a single terrace.

Outside the house attached to the Jellicoes' the front door was open, and a small boy stood in the light. His blond hair stood up in spikes, and he was wearing pyjamas decorated with dinosaurs. He held a plastic T-Rex in an unlikely shade of green in one hand.

"Dylan!" his mother exclaimed, appearing behind him. "You should be in bed."

"I saw the robber. I wanted to see if they would catch him," Dylan replied. "Like in my story." He looked up at Charlie. "Are you a policeman? Have you got a badge and handcuffs? Have you got a gun?" He turned the plastic dinosaur on its side and held it pointing forwards. "Bang! The robber is dead. Mummy won't let me have a real gun."

"Perhaps I could have a word with Dylan inside?" Charlie asked. "Only for a minute, because I think it's after his bedtime."

Charlie was shown into the front room. It had a three-piece brown leather suite, and a big TV on the wall, but everything else was child centred. There was a low plastic table with four matching chairs. The table was piled with drawing and painting materials, and there were shelves of toys and children's books around the walls.

"Sorry about the toy library," Dylan's mother said, "I'm a childminder. Dylan's at school though, aren't you, lovey?" She ruffled the boy's hair. By now Dylan was yawning, but the set of his chin said he wasn't going back to bed without a fight.

"Can I see your gun?" Dylan asked Charlie.

"Welsh policemen don't carry guns," he said. The boy looked disappointed. "We have pepper sprays and batons though. Sorry, but I didn't bring mine with me." An even more disappointed look was the result. "But," Charlie said, "I am a detective, and detectives need people's help. I need your help. Can you be a detective and help me?"

"Mummy says I can't have a gun," Dylan said sadly.

"Mummy says it's bedtime for little boys," his mother said, with a significant look towards Charlie.

"I can be a detective, Mummy," Dylan said, and Charlie thought that when you were six, anything was a better alternative to going to bed.

"OK then, Dylan," Charlie said. "You told me that you saw the robber. Where were you when you saw him? Could you show me?"

"My room. Can we show him?"

Dylan's mother stood up. "Come on then." She took Dylan by the hand and the three of them processed up the stairs and into the little room over the front door. There was only room for a single bed (with dinosaur bedding) and a built-in cupboard. The window overlooked the exact spot where Mags had been attacked. The little boy climbed up onto his bed so that he could point.

"That's where I saw the robber. Where that lady is." That lady was Patsy, fixing the blue tape around the crime scene.

"How did you know it was a robber?" Charlie asked.

"He had a robber's hat. With little holes." Dylan pointed to his eyes.

"That's great," Charlie said. "Did you see him before he put the hat on?"

Dylan nodded solemnly. "I was looking for dinosaurs," he said.

"He does that a lot," his mother said. "Though not always in the middle of the night."

"Was the robber bigger than me?" Charlie asked.

Dylan nodded. "Big as Daddy," he said. "But he had lots of hair like me and grandad."

Dylan's mother giggled softly. Charlie envisioned her husband, whom he'd met outside and who had a head as polished as a bowling ball. Under the streetlight it had shone.

"Same colour as your hair?" Charlie asked and Dylan nodded.

"Yellow hair," he said, and yawned.

"One more question, Charlie said. "What did the robber do before he put his hat on?"

"Stood still, like when we play statues. Then Aunty Mags came, and he put the hat on, and he tried to rob her. Is Aunty Mags alright? Are you going to catch the robber?" Excitement had been replaced by worry, and possibly fear.

Charlie crouched down in front of the little boy and looked him in the eyes.

"The police always catch robbers," he said, wishing it were true, but determined that Dylan wasn't going to be in any doubt and have nightmares about it. "Aunty Mags has gone to the hospital, and they will make her better. She'll be home tomorrow, and you can see her. You know Aunty Mags is a police officer too? So that means we'll catch the robber in double quick time. Won't we Mummy?"

Dylan's mother nodded. "We'll see Aunty Mags as soon as she gets home, lovey."

"Would you like a ride in a police car, Dylan?" Charlie asked, and all thoughts of robbers were banished in a huge grin.

"Can I, Mummy?"

"We'll see. If you go straight to sleep."

Dylan scrambled into bed and pulled the duvet up to his chin, squeezing his eyes tightly closed. Charlie tiptoed out of the room, leaving Dylan to his mother's ministrations. Dylan's dad was at the bottom of the stairs looking anxious.

"Is Dylan OK?"

"He's working hard on going to sleep on the promise of a ride in a police car," Charlie said. "But he saw what happened. I told him we'd catch the man who attacked Mags, and thanks to what he saw, I've got a good idea who it was. Are you related to Mags?"

Dylan's dad shook his head. "Honorary aunty. Is she OK?"

"He cut her arm, but I don't think it's serious. I think the hospital trip is about reassurance as much as anything wrong. She was protesting all the way."

Charlie left a card and asked if he could return to see Dylan again. "And I'm dead serious about the police car thing, if you think he'd enjoy it."

Dylan's dad laughed. "Only if I can come too."

"Deal," said Charlie.

21

Gate Street blues
TUESDAY 10.30PM

Eddy and Patsy were conferring by the police car when Charlie left Dylan's house. Eddy was clutching a handful of evidence bags.

"Sarge," Eddy said, holding up the bags. "Balaclava, gloves, knife. All in a restaurant bin. Worth taking a look for fingerprints on the lid, I reckon. I've taped it all up and put a sticker on it."

Charlie grinned. "Result. I've got a witness. A good one, if young, and I've also got an idea who did this. Who do we know who has bright blond hair, and an interest in making us think the flasher is still around?"

The other two looked blank.

"What about Harrington-Bowen? He's been sheltering Gwilym, and he fits the description. Gwilym said he thought his uncle knew about his activities with the knife and the mobile phone videos. I wonder if it was him following women police officers around... spreading confusion is his favourite thing."

"Could be," Patsy said. "But surely Mags would have recognised him?"

"He stepped out from behind her with his face and hair

covered and he didn't speak. He struck her with a knife and knocked her over. Whatever she says, she must have been terrified. We often don't recognise people out of context, and this was as out of context as it gets. But we need to ask her. Then we need a picture of Harrington-Bowen to show our witness, and we need to fingerprint the bin and get all that lot off to the lab for DNA."

"One more thing," Patsy said. "Under the wall there it's thick with leaf mould and mud. There are footprints, though not clear ones, but anyone who stood there for long is going to have that stuff all over their shoes."

"Did you get a sample?" Charlie asked.

Patsy gave him a withering look.

"Of course you did," Charlie said. "We need his clothes and his shoes. Tonight, before he washes them. And in an ideal world, his DNA. But we've got no grounds to insist. If we try to persuade him and he says no, then we've warned him. If we wait for more evidence and a warrant, he can clean up."

Eddy waved one of his evidence bags. "I don't believe anyone can wear a balaclava without leaving DNA on it. He was stupid to throw it away. I think we can wait."

Charlie nodded. At the very least there would be hair on the inside of the hat, and almost certainly saliva. Possibly Mags' own saliva, or even blood. There might be fingerprints on the bin. They were starting to make progress.

"We'll start again in the morning," he said. "Tomorrow's probably our last day without a big squad of Harrington-Bowen's friends arriving to take over, so we need to nail him. That's going to be easier after a night's sleep. We've caught the flasher, and the arsonist, so getting the murderer and whoever's behind the fraud is all in a day's work for us." Especially as Charlie was now confident that they were the same person, and he knew who it was.

22

Unexpected visitor
TUESDAY 11.15PM

How Charlie found his way back to Aunty Dilys's he didn't know. Today seemed to have lasted at least a week. He came close to tripping more than once because his feet felt weighted with lead. A shower, he thought, and then lots and lots of wonderful sleep. So, he wasn't pleased to hear his name called as he stepped through the front door. A familiar figure appeared in the hallway, and Charlie's heart lifted.

"Tom?" Charlie asked.

"Come and sit down," Tom said, opening the door to the residents' lounge. Twin black leather sofas and matching armchairs were arranged in a square around a smoked glass coffee table. The carpet was a deep grey, and the only colour came from the scatter cushions, which were liberally scattered. Dilys appeared to have bought a cushion every time she saw one she liked, regardless of colour or design. A sideboard held the makings of tea and coffee, and a plate of foil-wrapped chocolate biscuits. Tom had switched on a standard lamp by one of the armchairs, and the gentle light, after the buzzing fluorescents in the police station, was a balm for Charlie's aching head.

Tom was dressed in jeans and a dark purple sweater that

brought out the colour of his eyes. The room was warm, so he'd rolled his sleeves up, revealing enticing and half-hidden tattoos. There was an open book face down on one of the armchairs; Charlie saw it was something to do with expressionist art, whatever that was. Tom picked the book up and closed it. "I'm supposed to review the blasted thing. I don't like the pictures and the author can't write," he said.

"Why are you here?" Charlie asked. The words came out more sharply than he intended, but he was tired.

"Three reasons. First, I wanted to see you. Second, I want to tell you about the painting students, and third, I need to explain some things."

Charlie hadn't entirely given up his hope of a shower and sleep, but this was Tom. Off-limits, family-man Tom. Tom who talked about art and people, rather than about crime. Tom, whose life was not bounded by criminals and sexual assault and dirty cops.

Charlie took his coat off and sat down on one of the sofas, at right angles to Tom.

"Here I am, so that's one thing off your list."

"So you are," Tom said with a smile. "And my evening is all the better for it." He spoke with such sincerity that Charlie laughed.

"I haven't been having that effect on many people today," he said.

"You look exhausted," Tom said. "I'm sorry, this can all wait until the morning."

"Tell me about the painting students. Please tell me something solid that I can work with. Show me the money trail. Because everything else is nebulous and fucked-up."

Tom leaned forward in his armchair and picked up Charlie's hand. Charlie didn't stop him, because Tom's hand was warm, and large, and comforting. Tom's face was in shadow, but Charlie could smell the Old Spice and the scent of clean clothes.

"I can't give you anything concrete," Tom said. "I'm no more a detective than I am a college principal, but I did talk to the two painting tutors. I didn't want to say too much, so I pretended that there had been complaints about the quality of this year's intake, especially the new international students. They agreed with every word. Most of the new international students are keen as mustard, but none of them scream talent."

"How many are there, and what about the other disciplines?" Charlie scoured his brain for what the other disciplines might be. He thought 'making things with junk' probably wasn't a department. "Sculpture? Photography?"

"There are eight international students who came here intending to specialise in painting, including Kaylan and Rico. My colleagues say that the only one with any talent was Rico. The others are competent, and work hard, but nothing more. Both the tutors I talked to joined the College quite recently, three years ago if memory serves. They thought it was normal to have sub-standard international students,"

"If every one of them paid an extra fifty-thousand dollars …" "… and it had been going on for a few years …"

"Exactly my thoughts," Tom said. "That's why I wanted you to know. Not all the international students are from the US, so the amounts might be different, and sometimes we have more or fewer international students. If I can trust David from Finance, the college has never seen a penny of that money."

Charlie's mind was racing. It wasn't the Hatton Garden robbery, or Brinks Mat, but the fraud could be bringing someone, or several someones, getting on for half a million dollars a year, every year for at least the last three.

"The Pepperdines are on their way from Los Angeles," Charlie said. "We need to know exactly how that money was paid. Did it go into college funds and then disappear, or was it diverted before you ever got it? *Do* you trust David in Finance?"

Tom shrugged. "I don't know. I've been principal for a week. I don't *not* trust him, or anyone else. I just *don't know.* I have absolutely no idea what I'm doing. If it wasn't for you and Ann, I would have sat there in that office, wishing I was back in New York, and missed a major fraud, as well as more attacks on our students." He shook his head despairingly.

Without thinking, Charlie dropped to his knees in front of Tom and held his other hand.

"You're doing well from where I'm sitting. Being a better detective than me."

Tom smiled and winked. He had the most flirtatious wink Charlie had ever seen.

"I like where you're sitting," he said, and then held his hand out to stop Charlie getting up. "Wait a sec, there's something else, and it's probably made it all much worse."

"Go on."

"Vitruvious came in while I was talking to David. I didn't hear him, but he must have heard the tail end of the conversation. He went spare. *People come here to learn to paint, Tomos. Proper painting, not cartoon etchings.*"

"That would be you, then?"

Tom nodded. "Oh yes. I got the whole lecture. Painting should be *passionate* whereas I am merely whimsical. It should have a *message*, blah, blah. He's obsessed with the poetry of Byron and French Romantic painting. The clue is in the name: *Romantic.* I'm not against romance, or passion you understand, or indeed messages, but the public today don't get a *message* from nineteenth century oil paintings. I shouldn't let him rile me."

Charlie had absolutely no idea what any of it meant. It must have shown on his face.

"Sorry," Tom said. "You're not interested in my arguments with Vitruvious."

"Actually I am. I understand the individual words, but … I would like to know what it all means." Because Charlie found it all much more interesting than he expected. Also, he liked listening to Tom talk about things that mattered and that weren't sordid crime. He liked listening to Tom, full stop, and he was too tired to fight it.

Tom took a deep breath. "If you're sure?" Charlie nodded. "I'll show you." He got out his phone and fiddled for a minute. Then he handed it over. It showed an image of a woman holding a French flag, dress slipping to show her breasts, leading a rabble over a pile of dead bodies. In the background, a city appeared to be on fire.

"This is a painting by Eugene Delacroix: *Liberty Leading the People*, from about 1830ish. See, it's passionate, and conveys the message of the revolution: Liberty, Equality, Fraternity. All his pictures have lots of dead bodies, and passion and messages. They're all huge. Then there's Theodore Géricault, who Vitruvious almost worships." Tom fiddled with his phone a bit more and showed Charlie a picture of a group of dead and dying men, artistically draped over a raft made of planks of wood. Charlie thought it was revolting.

"*The Raft of the Medusa*," Tom said. "Painted a few years before the Delacroix. I don't know the full story, but it was a big scandal. Those men were basically abandoned by the captain of the Medusa and left to die."

"Hence the interest in small boats and refugees," Charlie said,

"Exactly so."

"This is the kind of painting Vitruvious teaches?" Charlie asked.

"It's the kind he *does*. Most people, including a lot of people who buy art, think it's old fashioned and, frankly, overblown. *The Raft of the Medusa* is sixteen feet by twenty-three for heaven's sake. If people want to have their emotions stirred, they probably go to a movie, or read a book. There's no room in something like these pictures for the viewer to decipher what they're seeing; it slaps you in the face like a wet fish. I mean, the painting itself is magnificent … but rightly or wrongly, popular it isn't. Admired, maybe, but not really liked."

Charlie grinned and leaned against Tom's legs. "There you go, giving both sides as usual." Then he remembered, and sat up. It felt good to lean against Tom. It felt right. But it wasn't right. Tom wasn't available, and they should both stop pretending he was.

CHARLIE LOOKED AGAIN at the picture of the *Raft of the Medusa*. He hadn't seen it the first time, but a tiny blob on the horizon could have been a ship in the far distance. Were the men on the raft trying to attract its attention? He asked Tom.

"Well spotted. That is indeed a ship, and the rafters were rescued, though if memory serves, most of them were already dead. There was talk of cannibalism. Like I said, I don't know the full story, even though it is a very important painting. Part of The Canon, as we say." He raised his eyebrows and pursed his lips. Charlie had no idea what Tom meant by *The Canon*, but from Tom's expression it wasn't something to be admired without reservations. He wanted Tom to keep talking, to explain what he meant. Charlie was tired, and his tiredness was messing with his judgement where Tom was concerned.

The guy was hot, he was interesting, and he was *married*. There was a fraud to investigate at the college, never mind a murder. Collusion between college authorities and the police had caused enough trouble. And he, Charlie, had already committed one massive error of judgement and had his face plastered all over the internet as a result.

"Thank you for telling me about it," Charlie said. "But it's been a hell of a day. I need to go to bed, but I will be in touch tomorrow." He started to get up.

"Wait a minute," Tom said. "There's something I want to explain."

Here it comes.

"I know. You're married. I don't sleep with married men," Charlie said.

Tom reached his hand out, and Charlie pulled away. "Every newspaper and podcaster in the UK made out I'm a slut who hooks up with anyone who asks after a few drinks. You need to get your head round the fact that I'm not."

Tom reached out again, and took Charlie's hand, ignoring the resistance. He leaned forward and caught Charlie's eye.

"Charlie. Listen for ten seconds. I. Am. Not. Married. I have never been married; I have no plans to get married. I have no romantic interest in women. I don't know who told you I was married, but they got it wrong. I'm a gay man who helped two lesbian friends have children. I have twin thirteen-year-old daughters. I help care for them. But the only relationship I have with their mothers is that one of them is currently my secretary."

Charlie stared at him.

"That's what I tried to tell you earlier. And as for the other stuff, I've been in New York, remember. I liked you before I knew anything about the trial. I like you. I like talking to you." Tom shrugged again. "That's it really."

The words burst out of Charlie before he could stop them. "I don't know anything about art. I haven't even got a degree. I'm a copper. One who's probably going to be unemployed soon. I'm a fuck-up. I'm sorry, Tom, but this can't go anywhere, and I really, really need some sleep."

In response Tom leaned forward and put his hands on Charlie's biceps. He pressed his lips to Charlie's forehead, then looked him in the eyes.

"I don't care about that stuff," he said. "I like you exactly as you are. I liked you when you were getting drunk in the Rainbow, and I like the way you've changed my thinking about the assaults. I don't know who you see when you look in the mirror, but I see someone I want to spend time getting to know. But if you don't like me in the same way, I'll leave you alone." Tom stood up, holding his hand out to help Charlie from the floor.

"I don't want you to leave me alone," Charlie said without conscious thought. Then he lifted himself onto his toes, put his arms round Tom's neck and kissed him. He felt warm arms around his shoulders, the brush of Tom's beard against his skin and he melted. Tom kissed him back and it was the best kiss ever. A kiss to make you lose track of time; a kiss to go on forever.

But it couldn't. Charlie had to sleep; he could feel the need dragging at his body. He pulled away, resting his head on Tom's chest, his lips tingling, and his body wishing things were different.

Tom held him close, and then let go.

"To be continued?" he asked.

Charlie nodded, and reached up for a last, quick kiss.

"But not tonight. I will be in touch tomorrow, though." Charlie needed one more day and he could unravel it, he was certain. And then maybe there could be something with Tom. Or more likely not.

Tom let himself out and Charlie went upstairs buzzing with… something. Happiness? Anticipation? Desire? Certainly desire. There was no future in it, he knew that, they were from different worlds, but he'd enjoy a bit more time listening to Tom talk about his work. He'd also enjoy seeing how far the tattoos extended … He couldn't hold the thought for long, he was too tired.

But he woke up in the night with something Tom had said nagging at him. It was the painting, he realised, the one with the people on the raft. He propped himself up on his pillows and fumbled for his phone, struggling to remember the name of the picture. He got there in the end and read the whole

Wikipedia entry. Turned out that artist had made a scale model of the actual raft after talking to two of the survivors. He'd also spent time in hospitals and mortuaries to accurately represent the dead and dying in paint. The people on the raft died of starvation and dehydration after the food ran out and the only two barrels of water were lost to the sea. But that was in eighteen hundred and something in France.

That wouldn't happen today. A painter who wanted to copy dehydrated corpses?

Would it?

23

Jared

Charlie walked to the police station determined to clear away all the detritus so that he could focus on Rico's death and the attack on Mags. In his mind, he ranked the different problems in order of importance, and those two were at the top of his list. He would go to see Mags later, and if she stuck to her story, and it held up with the physical evidence, and Dylan made an identification, they would be making an arrest. When they made it, Charlie was confident that the links between the police and the college management would be revealed. But right now, the fog of distraction stopped them seeing the connection. This morning, Charlie intended to get rid of the distractions in the same way that a gardener would clear brambles. First up, a call to Ravensbourne to get the forensic evidence collected and sent off to the lab, and then Jared Brody's computer hacking. He called Ravensbourne as he walked.

"We've got your flasher safely in the cells eating a police-special soggy bacon sandwich breakfast, and the custody officer says he's had a good night's sleep," Ravensbourne told Charlie. "If he tells us the same things that he told you last night, then the CPS will go for a charge on the assaults. Dunno about the arson, but I'll give it my best shot."

They arranged for the knife, balaclava, gloves and finger-prints to be sent to the lab.

"I'll put a rush on it," Ravensbourne told Charlie. "It's an attack on a police officer, so no argument that it's urgent."

The kettle in the break room was still warm, so Charlie wasn't surprised to see Patsy at her desk.

"I know how he sent the dick pics, and the pop ups about your court case," she said, as if reading Charlie's mind.

"Jared Brody?" Charlie said.

"Bring your coffee," Patsy said, pulling out a chair beside her. He sat where she indicated.

"I thought these computers had stopped working?" Charlie asked.

"I called in a favour from a guy in IT Support," she said, and blushed. Charlie had never seen Patsy blush but decided to say nothing. "He's a stay up all-night kind of person, so I came in early, and he was still at work. He had a good look round our system and found a little piece of software called *notey notey.* That's what Brody used. My mate says Brody must have by-passed the firewall and installed the software on all our computers. Once he'd done that, he could send pop-ups to his heart's content. My mate's cleaned it all up, and we now have regular, Clwyd Police-issue computers.

"By-passing the firewall sounds like something that shouldn't happen," Charlie said.

"Let's just say that my mate is taking that up with their boss."

Charlie sat back in his chair. The room was as dark as ever, so he could hear the buzzing of the fluorescent tubes hanging from the ceiling. Dust motes swirled in the air in the few rays of early morning sun that found their way through the grubby glass of the window. He thought about Tom getting anonymous pop-ups on his computer. Did that mean Brody had installed the software on those computers too? He asked Patsy.

"If the sender doesn't have the computer's actual address," she shrugged, "whatever that is, the pop-up arrives as an email. Once it's opened, it appears as a pop-up on the screen. My mate says a good hacker could install the software via such an email."

"What about the disappearing files at the college?"

"Completely different thing. And anyway, Sarge, Brody focussed on us, the Llanfair police. He wanted to embarrass women officers and to embarrass you in front of people you have to work with. That seems different to hiding a bunch of files at the college."

"Maybe," Charlie said. If the fraud was big enough, and it looked big, then Brody could be on the fraudsters payroll.

"We need to talk to Brody," he said. "Let's bring him in for a chat."

"He won't listen to either of us." Charlie wasn't sure about that. He might be the cop with his name in the papers, but he was sick of people assuming that because he was a not-very-tall gay bloke he was also a wimp. And Patsy was a whistle-blower FFS. Hardly the behaviour of a scaredy-cat. Which being so, he thought there must be something very unpleasant about Jared Brody.

"Patsy. Don't be daft. We're police officers. Get your coat. We might need Ravensbourne to give him an *order*, but we can ask him to talk." Brody had a large terraced house in the centre of Llanfair, only a five-minute walk from the station. It was still early, and Charlie liked the idea of disturbing their persecutor at his breakfast. Except they arrived at an obviously empty house. Peering through the front windows showed them a clean and tidy living room, without a mug on the coffee table or a TV remote control on the sofa to indicate that anyone had been there since it had been put straight.

Charlie and Patsy started knocking on doors. According to

the next-door neighbour, the Brodys had left two days ago, and they had no idea when to expect their return. "Took the kids out of school and everything," the neighbour said.

The neighbour on the other side said the family had relatives in Australia, and he thought that was where they'd gone.

Charlie and Patsy walked back to the police station Patsy insisting on taking a detour via the bakery for a bag of cookies.

"We need the sugar, to help us keep going," she said.

Eddy was waiting for them, his eyes lighting up when he saw the bakery bag. Patsy held it out of his reach. "Coffee," she said. Eddy disappeared downstairs with their empty mugs from earlier and reappeared a few minutes later with three full ones.

"What news?" he asked, once he'd taken the first bite from his cookie.

Charlie took a cookie and began to eat it. He wanted the others' reaction to his ideas, but he expected they would accuse him of madness. He wasn't sure they wouldn't be right. But he couldn't act without them, and they didn't have long. A cookie crumb caught in the back of his throat. He coughed to try to clear it, and then coughed some more. Eddy clapped him on the back, which did no good. The coughing continued until he was red in the face, and then suddenly the obstruction went.

"Sorry," he said. "Look. I think Vitruvious murdered Rico, and almost murdered Kaylan, and I think he's the one stealing the money from the college. But I can't prove it."

Eddy's rugby player's face held a look of scepticism, eyebrows raised, leaning one elbow on the desk with a cookie on the other hand. By contrast, Patsy merely seemed interested.

"I don't have any evidence, except some odd remarks, and not many of those. But they add up. We know Vitruvious is lying about who he is. His father is called Reinhard Volker, and Vitruvious doesn't acknowledge him. If we can believe Violet, they pretend they don't know each other because their politics are miles apart. We also know that Vitruvious is living in an expensive area, and drives an expensive car, though he's only getting his salary from the college, and according to Tom, no one wants to buy his paintings. Tom *is* a successful artist, and he's not making enough to give up the day job, so Vitruvious can't be paying for his house and car from painting."

"He could be living on credit," Patsy said. "Lots of people do."

Charlie nodded. "Could be. But last night Gwilym said that he'd heard Harrington-Bowen asking Vitruvious for money. *More* money. Harrington-Bowen has been protecting his nephew, to the extent of attacking Mags. I'm sure it was him, and I think he did it so that he could say the flasher was still around."

Eddy couldn't hold his scepticism back any longer. "Come on, Sarge. That's pushing it. If it was Harrington-Bowen, why choose Mags? Why not attack a student if he wanted to make it look real?"

Patsy gave Eddy a dirty look. "Because, stupid, Mags would fight back. If it was, HB, he wouldn't want to jerk off in front of someone, not for real. If it was him, and I'm not saying it was, he needed an excuse to leg it and not follow through."

Charlie breathed a quiet sigh of relief, but Eddy wasn't having it. "The MO is completely different. All the other attacks have been on women students on the campus."

This time Patsy kicked him. "No one knows that except us, Gwilym, and Mags. Because HB made damn sure that none of the details were properly recorded. The college wanted it all kept quiet, so only the Student Union had any records, and theirs weren't complete. Women police officers thought they were being followed. No one knew that the attacks didn't include non-students, because no one knew anything for sure."

"Maybe," Eddy still didn't sound convinced.

"I know it's far-fetched, but if Harrington-Bowen was being paid off by Vitruvious, and Gwilym knew, then Harrington-Bowen would have another reason to protect Gwilym," Charlie said.

"If." Eddy said.

Charlie rubbed his hand over his face, and through his hair. Faced with his inability to convince Eddy, his ideas sounded thin. Harrington-Bowen could have been protecting Gwilym because of their family relationship, but Harrington-Bowen didn't seem like that sort of man. On the other hand, Gwilym didn't seem sufficiently on the ball to realise that his uncle asking Vitruvious for money was something he ought to be keeping quiet.

"Yes, *if*," Charlie said. "But Gwilym did say that his uncle was asking Vitruvious for money, and he also said that his uncle was looking at having to sell his house. Your own research said the guy was broke. He's on divorce number three. So, we can assume that he needed money. People do strange things when they need money."

"Third divorce," Patsy said. "That's got to cost plenty. He's another one with a top-end car, and he spends a fortune on clothes. Inspectors don't get paid enough for brand new Range Rovers. I looked it up. I bet he's living on credit." She folded her arms, emanating satisfaction.

"OK," Eddy said. "Let's say you're right about Harrington-Bowen attacking Mags. Because we can prove that if forensics pull their fingers out. That doesn't explain why he was asking Vitruvious for money, or why you think Vitruvious murdered Rico. Or, come to that, why you think Vitruvious is stealing money from the college."

Charlie felt certain that Vitruvious was the murderer, and that he'd done it in pursuit of his painting. But it was a ludicrous theory, and the idea he was least excited about sharing. He hardly believed it himself. But theft? He believed that.

"The finance guy, David Something. He says there was no trace of the extra money coming into the college, but we have Michael Pepperdine's statement saying that he paid an extra fifty thousand dollars. I'd like to spend an hour asking the other international painting students if their parents paid extra. I spoke to Tom last night, and he said the other painting tutors were less than impressed with those students, so it's possible. Once we've got statements saying there was extra money paid, we can bring the finance guy in and get serious with him."

Both Eddy and Patsy were nodding. But Eddy had to spoil it.

"But how does that lead to Vitruvious being the murderer?" he asked.

"Duh," Patsy said, "Rico must have found out."

Charlie wasn't going to tell her that wasn't it. Because maybe it was. Maybe it was as simple as Rico Pepperdine discovering that his parents' money had been spent on Vitruvious's expensive lifestyle rather than the college. Baby steps, he thought. Let's just begin by proving Vitruvious was stealing the money.

24

Too nice to say so
WEDNESDAY 9AM

Armed with the names and room numbers of the remaining six international painting students, Charlie, Patsy and Eddy started knocking on doors in the hall of residence. Charlie started with Katy Malcovitz's room, and she answered the door in a pink silk dressing gown, blushing bright red when she realised it wasn't a fellow student. Her long dark hair was mussed from sleep.. Charlie produced his warrant card and the friendliest smile he could manage.

"There's no trouble, honestly, I just have a couple of really brief questions and I'll be out of your way," he said. "Five minutes, I promise."

"I guess that's OK," she said. "But should I have a lawyer?"

She hadn't opened the door more than a couple of inches, and Charlie had made sure not to crowd her. He heard the sound of someone else in the room; the sound of fabric against fabric, and the sound of feet hitting the floor.

"If you want a lawyer, that's fine," Charlie said, "but you truly don't need one. I'm not accusing you of doing anything wrong, but I think you can clear something up for me. You're potentially a witness, that's all." He smiled again until his cheeks ached. "We can go in the kitchen if you like, or down to the lounge, and I'm happy to wait while you get dressed."

The sounds from behind the door turned into a man's face over Katy's shoulder. The man's bed hair was more dramatic: the right-hand side stood up straight, while the left was pasted sweatily against his head. Seeing it made Charlie flatten his own hair in an unconscious gesture.

"Let him in, babe," the man said. "I've seen him around talking to the principal, and the cops don't have guns in this country. You don't have to answer anything you don't want to."

Charlie let a breath out. The man's accent was American; with luck, another painting student.

"Would you like a few minutes to get dressed?" Charlie asked.

Katy looked up and down the corridor. "It's fine, come in." She opened the door.

The room was the same as the two rooms he'd already seen. Tidier than Kaylan's, but not as tidy as Rico's. There was the same smell of oil paint, and the same pile of paint brushes and sketch books. Clothes lay neatly across the back of the desk chair. The duvet was thrown back on the narrow bed, and the smell of sex told Charlie that somehow, two full sized adults had spent the night together in it.

Without being asked, he sat down on the very edge of the armchair, making himself as small and unthreatening as he could, while signalling that he wouldn't be staying long. He waited until the man rested his arse against the desk, and Katy sat on the bed, tucking the gown under her legs and around her body and looking fractionally less worried.

"May I ask your name, sir?" Charlie said to the man.

"Sal Corbin," the man said.

Charlie smiled. "That's great, Mr Corbin. I was planning to speak to you as well. It's simple. I wanted to know how much you—or your parents—contributed to the college's special fund. I know that international students often make an additional donation, and I wondered if you had done the same."

"Why would you want to know that?" Sal asked.

"It's part of an ongoing investigation," Charlie said. "You should know there is absolutely no suggestion that there was anything wrong with those donations."

Katy's blush had faded, but it returned with full force. She wrapped her arms around herself. "My parents did make a donation," she said, looking sideways at Sal. "But they said not to talk about it. Not everyone can afford to pay extra."

Sal reached out and squeezed her shoulder. "Compared to what we could have paid in the US, this was a good deal. A degree only takes three years here, so they saved a year of tuition. My folks paid forty grand on top of the fees. I'm not scholarship material, detective, I'm just a lucky dude whose family had some good investments."

"I don't know what mine paid," Katy said. "But I know Dr Vitruvious talked to them about it. We don't discuss money. My mom told me they'd fixed it, and here I am." She tried a smile. It didn't come out very well, but given the way he'd interrupted her morning Charlie could only admire the effort.

Charlie stood up. "Thanks. That was all I needed to know. I might ask to speak to your parents on the phone later, but for now, that's it."

"Can we ask about Rico?" Katy said. "Because people are saying he was murdered, but no one is telling us what happened. He was a really nice guy." Her voice shook on the last few words, and Sal moved to sit next to her on the bed, his arm around her shoulders.

He looked up at Charlie.

"We, the painting students, wanted to do some kind of memorial. I know none of us have been here long, but…"

"I can't tell you anything yet, I'm sorry. When we can say

more, we'll be in touch with the college principal." Charlie hated having to retreat behind police-speak when these young people were upset. Murder did that. Spread shock and misery far beyond those immediately affected.

"Kaylan knows stuff," Katy burst out. "He was there, but he just sneers when anyone asks. When Sal suggested a memorial, he laughed and said there would be one though we would be too stupid to see it. I hate him." She clapped a hand over her mouth. "I don't hate him. I just wish he'd say…"

Charlie kept quiet, hoping for more. Nothing came.

"Thank you for talking to me," he said in the end, and let himself out.

As he walked down the corridor back to the stairs, he heard rapid footsteps behind him. He turned and it was Sal.

"Kaylan is a jerk, detective. We all think he knows something about Rico's death. Some people think he did it. Katy is just too nice to say so."

As AGREED, Charlie waited for Eddy and Patsy by the entrance to the hall of residence. He stayed inside, on a sofa by the window. Outside, the chilly wind had turned chillier, and the sun appeared only intermittently between the clouds. When the outside door opened, Charlie could smell rain in the air.

By contrast with the tiny window-slots in the student rooms, the reception area had large expanses of plate glass, allowing light to flood in, so that residents could see the doors to the lift, and read the numbers on the mailboxes. They could collect their mail in the light and then retreat to their dark cell-like rooms. Behind the lifts was a door to the canteen. Students came and went constantly. Each time the door opened, Charlie could smell bacon and coffee. But the door also let out the noise of a lot of people talking at once in a badly sound-proofed space, the clatter of tableware and the beeping of cash registers and card readers. After Dilys's bacon sandwich and Patsy's bag of cookies, Charlie couldn't summon any enthusiasm for food, or even coffee, not if it meant entering the maelstrom of noise beyond the canteen door. Instead, he relaxed on the couch and let his mind drift. Mainly he thought about kissing Tom, trying to ignore the voice in his head telling him that Tom was out of Charlie's league. Sometimes the voice was his own, sometimes his mother's. But the message was always the same: he wasn't good enough and he would get found out. After the events in Lanzarote, he doubted his own judgement. He had hooked up with a good-looking guy in a club, and that guy was tried for murder. He had given evidence in the guy's trial and his reward had been his picture all over the papers and social media. That he'd solved the murder and given the evidence to the local police counted for nothing. DS Charlie Rees was now *Gay Cop in Holiday Murder Scandal.*

He wrenched his mind back to the case, but the doubt had already worked its way into his thought processes. Yes, Vitruvious was stealing money from the college, with or without help from the finance department. But murdering a student so he could make a painting of the body? That was crazy talk. Just because some French painter had trawled the morgues for inspiration didn't mean a twenty-first century painter with a secure job would do the same. Géricault had made his name with *The Raft of the Medusa,* but Vitruvious was already well known. He was on TV. Students came from all over the world to study with him. Maybe he didn't sell many paintings, but…
The thoughts went round and round. It was bizarre, but it fitted. The two students had been dehydrated. Rico had been starving. Vitruvious was obsessed with painting desperate people on boats, pictures with a *message.* But Kaylan was alive and refusing to talk. No way would Kaylan be sticking up for Vitruvious if the tutor had tried to kill him. There was the coincidence of Kaylan appearing only a few miles from Vitruvious's old home, but Charlie couldn't read anything into that.

Vitruvious visited rarely, had even changed his name to distance himself from the place. No, they would tackle Vitruvious about the money, and see what happened. Charlie was so lost in his swirl of contradictions, that he didn't notice Patsy flop down next to him on the couch.

"Sup, Sarge?" she asked, and he came back to himself with a jolt.

"Sorry, miles away," he said. "Did you get anything?"

"Handcuffs for someone," she said. "Both of mine paid extra, both were in touch with Vitruvious before they came."

"Same," Charlie said. "We've got enough to talk to him under caution, whatever Ravensbourne says."

Eddy appeared at that moment and caught Charlie's words.

"Vitruvious? If he's not behind this lot, I'm about to be called up for Wales. What time do painting tutors start work?"

"Let's go and find out," Charlie said. As he stood up, his phone rang, Ravensbourne, with good news.

"We've charged your boy Gwilym with the assaults," she said. "Couldn't stop him telling us all about it. And the best outcome for Harrington-Bowen is a quiet resignation, because his nephew has dropped him right in it. *Uncle Nigel said it wasn't a crime, Uncle Nigel told me that if I didn't hurt them, it would be OK.*"

"Uncle Nigel probably attacked Mags last night," Charlie said. "I'm pretty sure he's involved in this fraud with Vitruvious as well. He should be prosecuted."

Ravensbourne didn't answer, simply sighed down the phone.

"Funny handshake brigade?" Charlie asked.

"Let's just say the powers-that-be may prefer that he disappears without a public fuss. And on another subject, you'll be reporting to Superintendent Kent after today. It seems he'll be back at this desk in the morning. That's partly down to you."

"Team effort, boss," Charlie said. "And now we're going to sort this fraud out." He felt a surge of confidence. Getting the flasher behind bars was a good result, and if the price was letting Harrington-Bowen keep his pension, he'd take it. It stank, but if Harrington-Bowen's Masonic brothers closed ranks, they'd struggle for a conviction even with the forensic evidence. That was how it was, and they did the best they could. Future women students were safe at least, and perhaps the previous victims would get some comfort from knowing that their attacker was in prison. He hoped so.

25

He's not there

On the way to the main building, the rain started. Huge drops, falling slowly at first, and then faster, until everyone, students and staff, townspeople and police officers, were running for cover. Charlie, Eddy and Patsy found themselves in the foyer of the library, hair plastered to their heads, shoes and trousers soaked. Outside the rain fell in torrents, washing piles of leaves into the gulleys and blocking them, until lakes spread across the tarmac of the paths and car parks. It streamed down the windows of the library, hammering on the glass and overflowing from the gutters in sheets of water.

"Coffee," said Charlie pointing at a machine near the door. "It'll give us chance to dry out a bit and to decide how we're going to play this. I think we need to talk to Vitruvious and the finance bod at the same time."

They found a low table and chairs and huddled over their coffee deciding who was going to do what.

"Vitruvious is trying to use his media contacts to keep us off his back," Charlie said. "If anyone's going to be accused of harassment, it should be me. My reputation can't get any worse. I'll talk to him, you two go and see what you can get from the finance guy."

Eddy and Patsy nodded and Charlie went on:

"We need formal statements from the parents, but given the number of students we've spoken to, we can act on the assumption those payments were made," Charlie said. "Either Vitruvious was acting alone, or someone in the college was helping."

They considered this statement of the obvious for a moment.

"And if they all deny it, sarge?" Patsy asked.

"Formal statements, interviews under caution with everyone who might be involved, however peripherally," Charlie said.

"Shouldn't you bring Vitruvious in for an interview?" Eddy said.

Charlie had been wondering the same thing.

"I'm afraid he'll go all *no comment* in a formal under-caution interview," Charlie said. "It's not that I think he's going to admit to anything informally, but he might let something slip if he thinks it's a conversation with someone not very bright, ie, me. There has to be some advantage in being *gay cop in murder scandal.*" Eddy blushed, and Patsy clenched her fists.

"It isn't fair," she said. "You *caught* the murderer."

Charlie shrugged. "I shagged him first." He stood up, still damp, but a bit warmer. "Let's go and catch some thieves."

The rain hadn't stopped, but it was no more than a fine mist when they stepped back outside. It was still enough to coat their hair, clothes and skin with droplets of water by the time they reached the main building. Eddy and Patsy asked for directions to the finance office and Charlie to Vitruvious's office. The receptionist showed Charlie some sheets of paper stapled together. "Second year Life Drawing," she said, "Dr V is supervising." She looked at the time on a big clock on the wall behind the desk. "There's forty-five minutes left, so go to the studio, not his office."

Charlie followed instructions to *climb the stairs to the next floor, turn left and it's the second room on the right*. Windows onto the courtyard lit the corridor despite the overcast day. The floor was dark wood planks, much stained though polished to a high gloss. The same dark wood panelled the walls to hip height. Above the panelling, the wall was painted white and hung with paintings, photographs, prints, and drawings. There were also several of what his college art teacher had called *collages*. All of it invited him to linger and look, but he had a job to do, and it wasn't art critic. He smiled to himself. A philistine, yes, but a newly interested philistine. Then he heard his mother's voice sneering at him for developing an interest in art when what he was really interested in was Tom. He silently told her to fuck off.

He opened the door marked Life Drawing to find himself facing a blank wall, with a heavy blue velvet curtain to his right, which made sense. Life drawing was drawing a naked model, so a little privacy was called for. It would be one thing to pose for artists, another to be peered at by every passer-by. Charlie pulled the curtain aside and everyone turned to look at him. Half the class turned away and back to their easels. He took a step forward. The model was a woman of about his age, obviously pregnant, standing with her arms folded against a classical pillar. She was resting her head on her arms, long hair obscuring her face. The pose was beautiful, and it was hard not to stare. There was no sign of Vitruvious.

"Who are you?" asked the student nearest to the door. "This is a private class." Charlie's eyes flicked to the student's drawing and *wow*. He wanted to study it and ask questions, but those weren't the questions he was being paid to ask.

"I need to talk to Dr Vitruvious," he said.

"Try his office," the student said, and turned away. There was nothing for Charlie to do but leave. Vitruvious's office was a bit further along the same corridor. Unlike the Life Drawing studio, the office door had an inset window, though it was obscured by sheets of paper roughly sellotaped into place. A small, engraved plaque next to the door read "Inigo Vitruvious, Snr Painting Tutor". Charlie knocked. There was no answer, and he had no sense that anyone was inside. He tried the door, but it was locked.

The office next to Vitruvious's had its door propped open with a rubber wedge. Charlie knocked anyway, and then entered. A woman with short purple hair was sitting at a table looking through a pile of sketchbooks. She saw him and started in her seat.

"Sorry, I was expecting my next student," she said.

"I was looking for Dr Vitruvious," Charlie said.

"Isn't everyone? I've already sorted his class out." She looked at her watch and jumped up. "Shit. Sorry, I've got to go and let the poor bloody model sit down before she gives birth from stress." Charlie moved out of her way and watched as she jogged down the corridor. He didn't have Vitruvious's phone number, or home address, but he knew a man who did. He set off for Tom's office, but before he had reached the stairs, Tom rang him.

"Vitruvious is in my office, Charlie, and he'd love to talk to you."

Charlie sincerely doubted it. But he was headed to Tom's office anyway, so he didn't hear the alarm that should have sounded in his mind.

Tom's office door was closed, and there was no sign of Ann in the outer room. Charlie knocked, and Tom called for him to enter.

Tom shouting through the door, rather than opening it himself, was the second cue Charlie missed, but opening the door without telling Eddy and Patsy where ha was going was the biggest mistake of all.

The noise he heard as the door opened sounded like the heavy-duty stapler his mother used to re-upholster dining chairs.

It wasn't.

It was Kaylan firing a pistol with a long barrel-shaped silencer in an enclosed space. Kaylan's arms were extended at shoulder height, both hands on the gun, and he looked like he knew exactly what he was doing. The bullet dug a hole in the wall next to the door, about a foot from where Charlie stood. It took him far too long to parse what he was seeing: Kaylan with the gun, Tom and Vitruvious with cable ties around their wrists and ankles securing them to two of the elegant conference table chairs. Navy blue cable ties, Charlie's brain noted, as if the colour mattered.

"Lock the door," Kaylan ordered. "Leave the key in it."

Charlie hadn't seen that the door had a key, but it did. A large key in shiny brass, entirely suiting the polished dark wood door. The door opened into the room. Charlie would need to remove the key, close the door and lock it from the inside. Instead, he threw himself sideways, out of the doorway and into Ann's office, expecting to feel a bullet tear into his flesh. Nothing happened. He pulled his phone out of his pocket and hit emergency.

"You can come in here and lock the door," Kaylan said calmly, "or I can start hurting people." There was the sound of something hard hitting something soft, and a cry of pain. "Like that," Kaylan said.

"Charlie, go," shouted Tom, which was when Ann and two other women appeared at the door to the outer office. He thought of Kaylan loose with a gun in a building full of civilians. There wasn't a choice.

"Get out! Armed man holding hostages!!" Charlie yelled. Then he stood up, grabbed the key, and had the door closed and locked with himself in the office almost before he had finished shouting.. He heard their agitated voices behind the door, and then he concentrated on what was in front of him. Nothing had changed, except that Vitruvious had blood running down his face. He and Tom were still tied to chairs and Kaylan was still pointing the gun at Charlie.

"What's going on, Kaylan?" he asked. "Let's stop this now, before anyone gets hurt. Put the gun down." Charlie knew from Kaylan's expression that it wasn't going to work. Then Vitruvious made it worse.

"I've been hurt. I've been stalked and threatened and robbed by this psychopath." For a man who had defrauded his own students of hundreds of thousands of pounds, Charlie thought Vitruvious sounded remarkably self-righteous.

"What's going on?" Charlie asked again.

"I'm going to kill that man, that liar and swindler," Kalyan said. "That so-called social conscience of the arts. And when I've done it, I'm walking out of here and you're going to let me. You're going to get me out of the building. If you try to stop me, I'll kill you and the principal as well, and anyone else who gets in my way. So, it's up to you."

The gun never wavered. Kaylan held it out in both hands as if he could keep holding it all day. His face showed no emotion, and for Charlie that was the most terrifying thing of all. Kaylan had a plan, and Charlie had no doubt that he would implement it unless he, Charlie, found a way to stop him.

"I don't understand," Charlie said. "You came halfway round the world to study with Dr Vitruvious. You told me you admired him."

Kaylan laughed. A forced, bitter laugh. The gun didn't move.

"He's not fucking *Doctor Vitruvious*. His PhD is another lie. Along with his concern for refugees, and his *authenticity*. Everything about him is a lie. Rico died for it and now he's going to die too."

"You killed Rico, you mad bastard. Don't try and pin that on me." Vitruvious strained against the cable ties, rocking to and fro on the chair, his eyes bulging, blood drying on his face.

"Listen to me policeman, Kaylan here killed Rico, killed the only decent painter I've taught for years. Starved him to death. He's mad, completely mad. Why don't the police come?"

"Shut the fuck up," Kaylan said. "The police are here, and they are going to watch me kill you and then they are going to help me leave." Kaylan never took his eyes from Charlie, but Charlie saw the tiniest tremor in Kaylan's right arm. *Keep him talking.*

"Kaylan, we can stop this. Put the gun down. Tell me what happened to Rico. Let's get some justice for him. He didn't deserve to die."

"Maybe he did." Kaylan said. "Some rich white kid from a nice first world home. Everyone turns out to get justice for Rico. No one cares about the thousands dying in the Texas desert, or drowning in the Mediterranean, or locked up in concentration camps, What about those people, Mr British Policeman?"

And now Charlie could definitely see a tremor in Kaylan's arms, and he could also see the madness in his eyes. Kaylan's mother's words came back to him. *He's always obsessed about something.*

26

From tiny acorns
WEDNESDAY 11.30AM

"I still don't understand," Charlie said, although he was beginning to have an inkling. "Mr Vitruvious is on the record as being very concerned about refugees. I've seen some of his paintings."

There was a grunt from Vitruvious.

"You might have seen them, Mr Policeman, but no one else has. I gave him the chance to show everyone what it means to suffer and die in the hope of a better life."

"Like Géricault? You wanted Vitruvious to paint actual dying people?"

"Ooh, an educated cop."

"But isn't that what you wanted him to do?"

"I gave him the chance of a lifetime. A painting that would shock the world. But he didn't care. All talk and no balls. Ask him about the money, go on ask him!"

"What money?" Charlie said. He wasn't taking his eyes off Kaylan. The gun was beginning to droop. Charlie could no longer see straight down the barrel.

"What money? The money *Comrade Inigo* has been siphoning out of college funds and spending on fast cars and hard drugs. *That* money. But he hasn't got it anymore, have you Comrade?"

And the final piece fell into place. The other thing Mrs Sully had said in her endless torrent of randomly mixed word salad. Kaylan's father ran the biggest cyber security consultancy in the mid-west and Kaylan *was good with computers.* Kaylan was the hacker. Kaylan had made the files disappear, and by the sound of it he'd been disappearing Vitruvious's money as well.

At the second *Comrade*, Vitruvious started shouting incoherently, rocking his chair and jerking his arms and legs. The louder he got, the wilder Kaylan's expression grew, until the air was charged with Kaylan's need to act, to fire his gun, to hurt and maim and kill. In Kaylan's version of reality, he had done what Vitruvious wanted and Vitruvious had thrown it back in his face. In Kaylan's distorted mind, Vitruvious deserved to die.

Charlie needed to act. He hoped Patsy and Eddy, and perhaps others, would know where he was. But he couldn't chance anyone trying to break down the door. Kaylan's arms might be drooping, but he could still shoot, and at this range he wouldn't miss. Charlie was desperate to look at Tom and Vitruvious, but he daren't take his eyes away from Kaylan. He needed a distraction.

By a miracle, he got one.

There was a crash and Tom's chair fell onto its side. At the same time the air filled with the scream of a personal alarm, deafening in the enclosed space. Charlie leapt for Kaylan, smacking the gun with his left hand and Kaylan's face with his right, as hard as he could. The two of them crashed into the table and fell on top of Tom as the alarm continued to shriek. Vitruvious screamed in competition. The noise was a physical entity, hammering at Charlie's ears, making it hard to move. He could smell Kaylan's sweat, Tom's Old Spice and something sulphurous that must be the gun.

His face was pressed against a table leg, and underneath him, Kaylan was a man possessed, lifting the gun as Charlie pressed it down with every ounce of his strength. It wasn't enough.

Kaylan fired.

Charlie felt the heat of the bullet, tearing his clothes, filling the air with the smell of burned cloth and skin, as a red-hot poker seared across his ribs and the underside of his left arm. He lifted his right fist and thumped Kaylan again in the face, feeling the crunch of a broken bone, and the spurt of blood from Kaylan's nose. But Kaylan still had the gun, and Charlie felt him move, his hand tightening to fire again. And underneath them both, Tom, tied to a chair, helpless.

Charlie saw the scene as if he were floating by the ceiling. Vitruvious thrashing and screaming, the back of his chair hitting the conference table, gouging and scratching the polished surface. Himself, blood seeping from under his left arm, trying desperately to contain Kaylan, and Tom, bigger than them both, unable to help, his shirt spotted with blood from Kaylan's battered face.

The alarm stopped, shocking Vitruvious into silence. In the quiet they heard voices outside the door, and the door itself rattling against the lock.

"Don't come in--armed man," shouted Charlie, and the rattling stopped. All he could hear was his own panting, as he tried to contain Kaylan, and Kaylan's grunts as he tried to escape. Vitruvious began to shout again, screaming obscenities until Charlie doubted his sanity. He could feel himself weakening, pain rippling out from his ribs, draining his strength. And then a crack, as loud as the gun, and another, and Charlie realised he wasn't fighting alone. A strong arm gripped Kaylan by the neck and pulled. Tom had broken the arms from the chair, and had his hand across Kaylan's windpipe, pressing down, hard.

Charlie dragged himself clear, scrambled to his feet and grabbed the gun, ignoring the pain in his ribs, as he kicked and wrenched until the weapon came free in his hands. Tom kept choking Kaylan, impervious to Kaylan's grasp on his arm as he tried to relieve the pressure. Charlie had handcuffs, and he used the last of his strength to peel Kaylan's hands from Tom's arm until he heard the click of the cuffs closing on his wrists.

"Let him go," he rasped, and Tom lifted his arm.

Kaylan dragged air into his lungs with an audible groan, tears mixing with the blood on his face. His neck was purple with bruising, and his chest rose and fell as the oxygen began to flow.

"Sharp knife in the box by the desk," Tom said.

It took Charlie a moment to work out why he would need a sharp knife. *Cable ties.*

He got the knife, and very carefully inserted it between Tom's ankle and the chair, sawing until the tie parted. Then he did the other ankle. Tom rolled onto his knees and stood up, then deliberately kicked Kalyan in the ribs. "Sorry," he said to Charlie, and then held out his arms, enfolding Charlie with his body. Charlie felt Tom tremble as the adrenaline receded. His own legs were shaky, and the pain in his ribs and arm was making him nauseous.

"Fucking put him down and let me go," Vitruvious yelled.

"No," Tom said. "You can wait."

Charlie walked stiffly to the office door and unlocked it. He saw that the bullet that had grazed his ribs had landed in the centre of one of the chocolate box paintings. He couldn't feel sorry about it. It might even have been an improvement.

First through the door were Eddy and Patsy, with a very anxious-looking Ann standing well back.

"You're bleeding," Patsy said.

"That's because he's been shot," Tom said. "He needs a hospital, or at the very least a doctor, and I need you to get that thing out of my office." Tom pointed to the gun, lying out of Kaylan's reach in the middle of the carpet.

"We've called firearms officers, and they will do what's required," Patsy said. "And for now, sir, your office is a crime scene, so we'll need everyone to leave."

Vitruvious decided this was a good moment to start yelling again, demanding to be released.

"That man has stolen thousands of pounds from this college," Tom said. "I want him arrested."

Eddy and Patsy looked between Tom and Charlie. Charlie suddenly needed to sit down before he fell. Shock, he recognised, but that didn't make his head stop spinning, or stop his body beginning to shake with cold. Tom must have seen the blood drain from Charlie's face, and produced a chair, pushing Charlie into it with gentle hands. Then he took his own jacket off and wrapped it around Charlie's shoulders. Tom's body had warmed the fabric, and in turn it warmed Charlie. He didn't think he could stand up, but he had to take charge.

"Patsy is right," he said, swallowing hard, because vomit was rising in his throat. "This room is a crime scene. We need transport for Kaylan here, plus I'd like somewhere private to talk to Mr Vitruvious. Tom will need to give a statement, and I need to make some calls."

Slowly, they got themselves sorted out.

With Tom's help, Charlie got out of the chair and into the corridor beyond Ann's office, where he sat on the floor and called Ravensbourne. She promised to be there within the hour, with a forensics team and some uniforms to boost their numbers. Eddy released Vitruvious and stashed him in an office next door, threatening him with handcuffs if he tried to leave. Kaylan was moved, none-too-gently, to Ann's office and was left to stew, which for once he managed without talking. There was no suggestion that the handcuffs were coming off before a nice solid cell door had closed behind him. Crime scene tape was plastered all around the door and corridors near Tom's office and the students and staff were sent home.

Patsy took a statement from Tom, and Charlie listened through the fuzziness in his head, the words providing a background hum as he waited for Ravensbourne to arrive and take charge. His ribs and arm were beginning to throb painfully enough that it was hard to think about anything else. He wanted to wrap himself more tightly in Tom's jacket but attempts to move sent his injured ribs into a spasm that he never wanted to repeat. What he wanted was to hand over to Ravensbourne and sleep for a week.

After an eternity, Tom came and squatted down in front of him.

"You need the hospital," Tom said. "You're oozing, and you've gone a very interesting shade of pale." He made to adjust the jacket so that it covered more of Charlie.

"Don't touch. Please." Charlie said, trying to keep as still as he could. "I can't leave, not yet."

"Waiting for an SIO? See, I remembered."

"She's on her way." Charlie knew Tom was trying to make him smile, but he couldn't summon the energy. "What happened before I got there? In your office, I mean?"

"Short version: Vitruvious came to complain about Kaylan essentially stalking him, I said he brought it on himself, he lost his temper, and we were having a row when Kaylan appeared with that gun hidden under his hoodie." Tom paused. "He might be a psychopath, but he's a clever psychopath. He made me tie V to the chair, and then he said he'd shoot V if I didn't fasten my own ankles to the chair, and one wrist. Then he did the last one. He held the phone while I talked to you. The rest you know. How much longer is this woman going to take?"

"What about that rape alarm?" Charlie wanted to know, but it was hard to get the words out. Shivery was the only word that seemed to fit, except he wasn't moving. He didn't dare move.

"That was dumb luck. It was in my pocket, and I must

have fallen on the button. I was watching you watching Kaylan. I don't know what happened, but your eyes changed, and I thought you were going to jump him. I thought I'd see if I could provide a distraction."

Charlie remembered that Kaylan's arms had begun to tremble, but he couldn't get his mouth to form the words. His eyes closed. He was hot and cold at the same time.

"Charlie. Stay with me. Look at me, Charlie. Don't go to sleep."

Why not? I want to. I don't think I have a choice.

He drifted in and out of the pain.

And with a noisy rush, the paramedics arrived, loaded down with bags the size of small cars.

A minute after that, everything faded to a blissful black.

27

Awake
THURSDAY 8AM

Charlie opened his eyes, then closed them again. The light was bright, but the sheets were clean, and the pillow dented in just the right way. The cotton felt good against his skin; stiff with starch but also smooth with the softness that came from multiple washings. He was warm. He drifted. Sometime later he opened his eyes again and heard someone say his name. The someone was a nurse, and he couldn't pretend he was at home in bed, with a day of nothing to do stretching out in front of him.

"Hello," he croaked.

"Let's get you sitting up," she said, making the head of the bed tip up, so that like it or not, he could see his surroundings: a pale green hospital room, with the usual drip stand, wash basin, chairs in wipe-clean fabrics and a bedside table with a box of tissues, a covered water jug and a plastic beaker.

"How's your side?" she asked, sticking a thermometer in his ear.

"Sore," he said. "My arm too."

"Temperature fine." She noted something on the chart hanging on the end of the bed. "Blood pressure." She pumped the cuff up round his uninjured arm and noted that down too, tested his oxygen level and his pulse and noted them without sharing. "I'll bring you some painkillers," she said and left.

Charlie looked down at his body. The whole of his left side was covered in dressings, as was the top of his left arm. They both hurt. The bandages on his side were stained with blood, and he didn't want to know what was underneath.

The nurse came back with a tiny plastic pot containing two tablets. She poured him a glass of water and held the pot out for him to take the tablets.

"Paracetamol," she said. He swallowed the tablets with some difficulty, because his throat was dry, and the tablets seemed huge.

"Right," she said. "Let's have a look at that dressing."

"You can look," Charlie said, "but don't expect me to."

She laughed. "It's not so bad. Lots of blood last night but keep it clean and you'll heal in a week. Turn on your side."

He turned and concentrated on his breathing as an antidote to worrying about what was under the bandages.

"No sign of infection," the nurse said. "We'll give you some antibiotics just in case. Take a couple of paracetamol three times a day if it hurts, and the district nurse will come and change the dressing. As soon as you've got some clothes and your prescription, you can go. There's an odd-looking woman, smells of cigarette smoke, wanting to see you, says she's your boss?"

Charlie grinned. "Yep, that's her."

The nurse gave him a questioning look and left, to be replaced by DCI Ravensbourne.

"Boss," Charlie said. "Sorry about this." He waved to indicate the hospital room, and his own incapacity. "They say I can go as soon as I've got a prescription. And some clothes." He looked down at the hospital gown and pulled the blankets a bit higher. He wasn't sure he wanted to share his half naked chest with Ravensbourne.

"Apologies, Charlie? You've singlehandedly solved crimes we didn't even know had been committed. You need a medal, boy." Her tone was light-hearted. Then she sat in one of the visitors' chairs and looked at him more seriously.

"We've got Vitruvious, Kaylan Sully and Gwilym Bowen locked up. I understand that Nigel Harrington-Bowen delivered his resignation letter to the Chief Constable this morning. Jared Brody is on holiday, but I expect he'll resign too. David Smith, who is the Chief Finance Officer at the College of Art has been suspended pending an enquiry. Michael Pepperdine has identified his son's body and given us a statement about the extra fifty-thousand dollars he paid to get Rico a place here. Gwilym will be charged with the assaults. We'll work on the arson, but don't hold your breath."

"What about the others?" Charlie wanted to know.

"That's where it gets interesting."

Charlie wasn't sure *interesting* was the word he would use, not while he was bandaged up in a hospital bed, with a gunshot wound, albeit a minor one.

"Surely we can get Vitruvious for the fraud at least?" he asked.

"Possibly. It depends on this David Smith. Pepperdine's paperwork shows he paid the money into the regular college accounts. If Vitruvious stole it, he must have had inside help. But there's no sign of the money anywhere. Someone has been very creative with the books. Vitruvious himself began by accusing Kaylan Sully of stealing, and then denied everything and anything. He's got himself a good solicitor, and I expect he'll be released pending enquiries later today. If David Smith coughs, we might get him, otherwise it's going to be a long slog."

"But Kaylan as good as admitted he'd made the money disappear." Charlie said. "He was taunting Vitruvious about it."

"It appears that Kaylan is a much cleverer young man

than he appears—at least where computers are concerned. Where guns are concerned, not so much. We've charged him with shooting you, and with kidnapping Tom Pennant and Vitruvious. But he's not talking. *We've* been talking though. To the Chicago police, and Kaylan's High Schools, plural. He has a sealed juvenile record according to the Chicago police. He was expelled from one school for stalking his history teacher and posting compromising photographs of him online. He was expelled from a second one for hacking into the school computer and creating chaos. In that case, the school's bank accounts were emptied, and the money has never been recovered."

"He wasn't charged with any of this?"

"If they could prove it, our Kaylan would be in a very secure prison somewhere in the USA with no access to the internet. But they can't. I'm going to be talking to the FBI later, because the Chicago cops said the FBI were very interested in young Sully. There's also the matter of where he acquired a gun and a silencer."

"You're saying he might get sent back to the states?" Charlie asked.

"He shot a police officer. He's not going anywhere until he's done his time for that. Which brings us to Rico Pepperdine."

"I'm guessing neither Vitruvious nor Kaylan is admitting anything about Rico's death?" Charlie asked.

"Not a single word."

There was a commotion outside the door to Charlie's room. The nurse he had been talking to earlier opened the door and slid in, closing it behind her.

"It's like Piccadilly Circus out there," she said. "There are two giants arguing about who gets to drive you home, and would you believe a couple of reporters? How they all got in, I have no idea."

"I'll sort it out," Ravensbourne said, and followed the

nurse into the corridor. The commotion stopped instantly, to be replaced with the insistent sound of Charlie's phone. He found it in the little cupboard under the bedside table, by which time it had stopped ringing. It had been a call from his mother. Her latest explanation of Charlie's character failings could wait, possibly forever. The little cupboard also contained what was left of his clothes: all bloodstained except for the socks; the shirt and sweater hanging in shreds. He was contemplating the underwear when he heard the door open, and dived back under the sheets, wrenching his wound and wishing he'd had the sense to move slowly. But it was Ravensbourne, and she didn't need to see him dressed in a hospital nightie.

"The giants are Tom Pennant and Eddy. I'm taking Eddy back with me," she said, "so you get Tom Pennant. I've told the reporters that if I see either of them one more time, they won't be invited to any Police Clwyd press conferences ever again."

She left and her place was taken by Tom, looking tired, but no longer spattered with blood. He had a small hold-all.

"Clothes," he said. "I went to see Dilys, and we found you some clean things. I brought one of my zip-up fleeces though, because I thought you wouldn't want anything to touch the wounds." He put the hold-all on the bed, as if he wasn't sure he'd done the right thing.

"Thank you so much," Charlie said, because the thought of putting on any of the bloodstained clothes was revolting. It was bad enough that he couldn't have a shower; he smelled of sweat and blood and something hospitally. Someone had done their best to clean him up, but there were still bits of dried blood on his skin.

"Do you need a hand?" Tom asked, and Charlie shook his head. The idea of getting naked in front of Tom wasn't abhorrent, but not like this.

"I'll wait for you outside," Tom said.

Charlie did need a hand, or ideally several, because almost any movement set his ribs twanging, and he had the horrible feeling of sore skin rubbing on sore skin. By sitting on the chair, he got socks, underwear and jeans on, and his good arm into the sleeve of the oversized fleece. The other arm and his shoes were beyond him. He shuffled over to the door and peered round it. Tom stood leaning against the far wall.

"Help," Charlie said, and Tom smiled. Tom always seemed to smile at him. In a good way.

For such a big man, Tom was gentle. There was no way Charlie could bend his arm backwards to get it down the sleeve, so Tom, pulled the fleece until it was in the right spot to slide into place. The shoes were no problem.

"I collected your prescription," Tom said. "We can go. Dilys wants you back at hers, though I said I have a spare room. She doesn't appear to think that I can look after you properly, and maybe she's right." Charlie saw Tom blush. "The thing is, my predecessor, Sir John of the hideous miniatures, has resigned, and the Governors have asked me to stay on as principal."

"I hope you agreed," Charlie said.

"I'll need to go back to New York for a couple of days to pack up my things, but otherwise yes. I made them promise to redecorate the office as a condition though."

As they talked, Tom led Charlie through endless hospital corridors until they reached the entrance with its card, magazine and gift shop, florist, coffee bar, and racks of leaflets about all manner of illnesses.

"Do you want to wait here, while I get the car?" Tom asked.

"No way," Charlie said. He didn't want to be inside the hospital for a second longer than necessary. "I can walk, I just can't bend. The difficulty isn't going to be getting to the car, it's going to be getting into it."

And so it proved. Luckily it was a smallish Renault SUV,

so Charlie didn't have to bend too far, and Tom did the honours with the seatbelt.

"Thanks," Charlie said, and then, "how are you doing? You must have some bruises, at the very least. Being kidnapped and threatened by one of your own students is hardly an everyday thing for an art tutor."

Tom concentrated on driving until they were out of the hospital and onto the road back to Llanfair.

"I can't pretend I slept well last night," he said. "But what I mostly am is angry. I didn't like Vitruvious before, but I bloody listened to him whine about being stalked, which only goes to show what a sucker I am. And then the stalker turns up waving a fucking gun."

He went quiet and concentrated on driving once more, though there was little traffic, and the road was almost straight without roadworks or potholes.

"I thought he was going to kill all of us. I can't stop thinking about it. You just stood there, talking to him, as if it was no big deal, while he pointed a gun at you. I did nothing."

"You gave me the distraction I needed," Charlie said.

"I closed my eyes. I thought he was going to shoot you, and I was too afraid to look. I hid, like a coward."

28

The right training
THURSDAY 11AM

Outside the car, the fields were green from the recent rain, and the muddy-brown river flowed swiftly, swollen with run-off from the hills. Clouds scudded across the sky, letting the sun break through and light up the turning leaves on the hill-side forests. The sides of the road ran with water, but the bigger floods had drained away. It was Wales in autumn, and it was beautiful. Charlie didn't think of himself as sentimental about his country, but the familiarity kept him grounded. He liked seeing new places—would happily take any opportunity to travel—but he couldn't imagine living anywhere but here. There was something about the endless variations on the colour green, the hillsides covered in trees and the red kites circling overhead, that slowed his heart rate and calmed his mind when things had been out of control. Things had been out of control for a while now, so he watched the landscape pass and considered what to say to Tom.

"The thing is, we're all cowards," Charlie said in the end. "You were stuck in a room with an emotionally unstable man with a gun who had tied you to a chair. There's no way to feel OK about that. The reason I could stand still and keep talking is down to training, not character. And you didn't panic, which *is* down to character. You probably saved my life. All our lives."

Tom took a hand off the wheel and took hold of Charlie's good hand.

"Thanks for saying that, even if it's not true. I'm going to be a real man about it and ignore all the feelings."

"You're an artist," Charlie said. "Aren't artists allowed to have feelings?"

"In moderation," Tom replied. "Provided that we can intellectualise them."

"That's better than coppers. Coppers aren't allowed to have feelings at all."

It seemed to Charlie that they weren't talking about any old feelings, and that once again he was saying things to Tom that he hadn't said to anyone else.

"Before I arrived," Charlie said, changing the subject before he found himself saying anything he might regret, "did either Vitruvious or Kaylan give you any clue about Rico's death? Because that's what's making *me* angry. Rico died, and one of those two is responsible, but so far, we don't have a case against either of them."

Tom frowned. "What do you think happened?" he asked.

"I think one or both of them had the idea of Vitruvious painting Kaylan and Rico as dying refugees, adrift at sea. Kaylan said it was a chance for Vitruvious to get attention to his work. Maybe they were going to talk about the experience of being starving and dehydrated as a publicity stunt to promote the picture. You said Vitruvious is good at getting media attention. I know it sounds bonkers, but Kaylan and Rico *were* dehydrated, and the post mortem on Rico said he hadn't eaten for days."

Charlie sighed. Saying it aloud made the idea sound even more ludicrous.

"And then it went too far, and Rico died?" Tom asked. "An accident?"

"The alternative to an accident doesn't bear thinking about," Charlie said. "Unless one of them talks we'll never know. They're both going to prison, but neither of them for Rico's death. No one is going to believe in my stupid painting theory. Vitruvious will probably get bail, dammit, and if he pleads guilty to the fraud, he'll get a nice open prison as a non-violent offender."

"So, we have to find the painting," Tom said. "Or rather, we have to find the sketches. Because if you are right, and Vitruvious was emulating Géricault, studying the dead and dying in order to shock his audience, then there will be sketches. Lots of them. Find the sketches and we'll have a record of what happened. Remember that he might be a monster, but Vitruvious is a good painter, and good painting is built on good drawing. He will have spent a lot of time drawing his subjects, and maybe photographing them too." Tom paused, frowning. His speed dropped until the car was dawdling along. A few other cars flew past, engines revving.

"Pull into that picnic area," Charlie said. "Because you obviously can't drive and think."

Tom grinned and turned up a steep track into a gravelled car park with paths leading into the nearby forestry and a couple of ancient picnic tables. He parked. There were trees all around them, mostly conifers, with their intense smell. Dead needles and pine cones littered the ground.

"Let's walk a bit if you're up to it," Tom said.

"Can you walk and think? Because if you can, I'm always up for some fresh air."

Tom helped him wriggle out of the car without too much pain, and they set off up the nearest path. A few hundred yards from the car, a disintegrating bench gave a view through a gap in the trees, across the river valley to the mountains beyond.

"I know red kites aren't such a big deal any more," Tom said, "but I love to watch them, and this is a good spot."

Charlie sat down carefully, but with some relief. Moments later, a fork-tailed raptor drifted into view, floating effortlessly on unseen currents, adjusting its trim by moving a single feather. As they watched silently, the bird was joined by others rising and falling, circling, speeding up and slowing, and always staring intently at the ground below. Charlie could feel the heat from Tom's body as they looked at the birds, and he himself in their endless movement. He wanted to feel Tom's arms round him, to tip his head up and find Tom's lips with his own. Tom leaned closer, and Charlie knew that he wasn't the only one feeling the possibilities charging the particles in the air between them.

Their lips met and Charlie melted into Tom, pain forgotten in the warmth, and, yes, desire. Tom's beard felt soft against his own stubbly cheeks, and then Tom's big hands were cupping his face and his dark eyes were gazing into his own. He broke the kiss and leaned back a little.

"That Eddy, the police officer," Tom said, "suggested that he might have some kind of claim on your person. I wondered if I'd got this wrong, but I don't think I have."

"You haven't," Charlie said. "I've no interest in Eddy, except as a colleague …" Charlie shrugged, and then winced as a spasm of heat and pain gripped his ribs. "Fuck."

Tom held his good hand until the spasm passed. Charlie was suddenly too cold.

"Can we go back?" he said, and Tom held his hand all the way back down to the car. Charlie didn't want to think about how much he liked Tom, because Tom was now a college principal, and he was a copper with his name all over the internet. So he thought about Vitruvius and where he might have left his sketches.

"DID YOU GET CHANCE TO THINK?" Charlie asked when Tom switched the engine on and revealed the heated seats.

"I mostly thought about you," Tom said, "and I'll be coming back to *that* issue later. But I've also been thinking about V's sketches. If we're right and he was drawing Rico and Kaylan over several days, those sketches are going to be incriminating. But they're also going to be precious. He ought to get rid of them, but he won't. I don't think I've ever got rid of a single one of my sketchbooks. The easiest place to hide sketches is with other sketches, so they're most likely in his studio at the college."

"Not wherever he kept Kaylan and Rico? Or at his house?"

"One of the advantages of working at the college is we get to use the facilities. He has a studio near his office. He would want the sketches with him so he could keep working on them."

"OK. His studio then. Ideally before he gets bail."

Tom put the car into gear, then paused. "You want me to come with you?"

"Of course. You think I'd recognise what I'm looking at?"

"Actually, I do. But that doesn't mean I don't want to help."

They were only a few miles from Llanfair, and Tom concentrated on his driving. When they reached the college, he parked in the space marked Principal and helped Charlie out of the car.

"Sir John drove a vintage something-or-other, and I'm sure people expect me to upgrade now I've got the big job. But my humble Renault is fine for me." Tom smiled. "Let me get a Campus Services Officer to unlock the door for us."

VITRUVIOUS'S STUDIO was exactly what Charlie had imagined an artist's studio would look like, only more so. One wall was almost entirely glass—a window looking out on to the court-yard, from a different angle to Tom's office, but no less lovely. Canvases with pictures more or less completed stood on easels, hung on the high, white-painted walls, or were stacked against every vertical surface. On the wall at the far end, away from the door, were shelves filled with sketchbooks, and rolls of grubby-looking paper, plus a plan chest, with its big flat drawers and a filing cabinet. There was a stained sink, the draining board scattered with used cups and empty glass jars. The middle of the room was filled by a huge table covered with more glass jars, cans stuffed with paintbrushes and dozens and dozens of tubes of paint. There were plates and saucers that appeared to have been used to mix colours, piles of rags, a big can of something called 'gesso' and a mixture of the kind of junk Charlie had seen in Violet's workshop. Around the table were three decidedly vintage stools, and by the window, a couch, with a set of overalls hanging over one end. Everything from the door handle to the sofa cushions was covered in blobs and smears of paint. Charlie couldn't help running his finger over the table, feeling the textures of dried paint which must have taken years to build up, layer upon layer, blob upon blob.

The smell of paint filled the air.

Charlie took in the few finished paintings. All were of the sea, some with boats, some with the shadowy figures like the one Tom had showed him in the library. He walked closer to a picture of a small boat being tossed about on huge waves.

"I've seen one of these before. Part of a series?" Then he laughed. Tom looked puzzled.

"IV," Charlie said. "The night I met you I slept in my car. In the morning, a kind man took me in and gave me some breakfast. He told me to stay with Dilys, rang her up. Anyway, he had a painting very like this, and he said it was number four in a series… which he knew because it had the Roman numerals IV on the back. IV. Inigo Vitruvious."

Tom nodded. "That's what he paints. You can see. He does portraits as well, but mostly seascapes."

Charlie realised that he didn't have any gloves, or evidence bags, or any of the things he usually had stuffed in his pockets. If the sketches were here, he needed to make this a legal search. "Wait," he said, found his phone and called Ravensbourne. "I think we can find evidence that Vitruvious was complicit in Rico's death," he told her, and explained about the studio in the college. "Tom, as college principal, has let us in."

"Do it," Ravensbourne said.

"If we find anything, touch it as little as possible and put it on the table. I'll clear a space." Charlie said. "I don't know what we're looking for exactly, though I guess I'd recognise Kaylan if not Rico."

"It's mostly going to be seascapes," Tom said. "We could pull out all the possibles and go through them together. You do the plan chest, and I'll start on the shelves."

The plan chest was a bust. Hundreds of sheets of paper of different weights, textures and colours filled the lower drawers. The top drawers held Vitruvious's work: a vast range of still life, the nude model he had seen in the life drawing class, drawings of boats of all shapes and sizes, and studies of the sea and the coast. But nothing even approaching pictures of Kaylan or Rico.

Tom was systematically opening sketchbook after sketchbook, flipping through the pages and replacing them on the shelves. Charlie had little knowledge of what Vitruvious used to draw with; charcoal? pencil? pen? Whatever it was it was transferring itself to Tom's hands, face and clothes as an all-over black dust. As Tom seemed to have a system, Charlie decided to start on the filing cabinet. That was a bust, too. Despite the mess of paint blobs and dust, Vitruvious kept his work in good order. The cabinet held files of newspaper articles, printouts from the internet, leaflets, government reports, exhibition catalogues, and pages and pages of handwritten notes. All of it was meticulously labelled: refugees-Libya, refugees-Mediterranean-rescue boats, refugees-English Channel-UK Govt policy, and so on. The files held what it said on the labels.

"Nothing," Charlie said. His side ached, and he was ignoring the feeling of blood seeping underneath the bandages. He'd been working one-handed, and now his uninjured hand and arm ached in sympathy. He was dirty and sweaty and he had a headache from the smell of paint. He sat very gently down on the couch by the window and wished someone would bring a cup of coffee and a sticky bun. Five minutes later, Tom joined him, looking equally dishevelled and dispirited.

"He must have them at home," Tom said.

"I'll need to get a warrant," Charlie said. "We'll get one, but probably not until after he's moved them somewhere else."

"It was worth a try," Tom said. "Though part of me hopes your theory is wrong. He's a hell of an artist. Those sketchbooks are fantastic."

"Hold that thought for when the papers get hold of the cash-for-places story," Charlie said, and slid down on the sofa to rest his head on Tom's shoulder.

From which angle he could see the large cardboard folder taped to the underside of the table.

29

Found

THURSDAY 1PM

Tom crawled under the table, photographed everything and unstuck the folder—no more than two sheets of card tied together with string, encasing a series of drawings. They cleared a space on the table and opened the folder. The drawings began with portraits of Kaylan and Rico. Charlie hadn't seen Rico in life, but he had seen a lot of Kaylan, and Vitruvious had captured him perfectly. As well as portraying Kaylan's appearance, Charlie saw Kaylan's sense of entitlement and his disdainful arrogance. Charlie stared at one image in particular. It showed the Kaylan he had seen yesterday, the man who could hold a gun steady, and who could threaten to use it so believably. Vitruvious had seen that in Kaylan and had the talent to put it on paper. By contrast Rico had a gentle face. Vitruvious had drawn him as sweet and innocent, quiet and thoughtful. From these pictures, it wasn't hard to see why their fellow students preferred Rico to Kaylan.

"I want to photograph each one," Charlie said, and they moved things off the table so Charlie could get a reasonable picture on his phone.

Charlie and Tom turned the pages. More portraits of the

two students. As the series progressed, their clothes became creased and dirty. Their hair lost its style, and stubble showed on their faces. Lack of sleep showed as dark rings beneath the eyes.

Halfway through the pile of drawings things changed still further, and not for the better.

"They're suffering," Tom said, looking at the two faces with horror. "They're ill. He must have stopped giving them anything to drink. I looked it up. You can go weeks without food, but you have to keep drinking."

"If it's hot, dehydration kills in a couple of days," Charlie said. He knew what was coming. Rico was going to die, and Vitruvious's meticulous drawings would record his death, and the decay of his body.

They stood with the pile of drawings in front of them on the table, staring at an image of Kaylan, with sunken, haunted eyes and chapped lips. Everything about him looked dry, almost desiccated.

"We did lock the door?" Charlie asked and Tom nodded. "I'm going to ring Ravensbourne, and then I want you to go and sit down while I photograph the rest. It's my job. You shouldn't be here at all." Charlie knew he should send Tom out of the studio, but he couldn't make himself do it. He needed to know there was a sane, kind, living person in the room with him. Which didn't mean he was going to let him see those drawings. Tom was having enough nightmares already.

Ravensbourne listened for thirty seconds and said, "I'll ring you back. Don't leave." Charlie carried on turning the pages and taking photographs. Tom didn't move from his side, despite what Charlie had said, and Charlie was glad of it. As the series continued, Rico was pictured naked but for his shirt. Tom ran a finger over the gentle face, sometimes shown with closed eyes, and sometimes with his hands held out in supplication and his face crying out for relief. The drawings shrieked of despair and the knowledge of impending death. Charlie tried not to look as Rico's life dimmed and then ended. With horror, Charlie saw that Rico's dead body had been *posed* as it lay to suggest that it was hanging over the side of a boat. In another image, a background of water and a pebbled beach were sketched in around limbs stiffened and swollen. In yet another, Kaylan was posed as if leaning over something, or someone. Tom put one picture above the other and Charlie could see that together, there would be a drawing of one man tending to the dead body of his friend. The drawings were brilliant, and perhaps that was the worst part of all.

As Charlie photographed, he focussed on a single line or two, letting the rest blur as he clicked. His tears, and Tom's, fell freely, their hands wiping them away to keep the pages clean. By the time he'd finished, Ravensbourne still hadn't called back. He left the drawings, all now face down, on the table, and went to sit with Tom on the sofa.

There was nothing to say. His throat held a stone blocking him from speaking, a stone that would burst into a flood of howling despair if he tried to utter a word. He sent all the pictures to Ravensbourne, with a warning, and they waited, holding onto each other as a barrier against the evil in the room. Tom said, "Vitruvious would never have been able to show these. Even he must have known that."

Charlie shook his head, as he struggled to get the words past the obstruction in his chest. "You're wrong. I'm sorry, Tom, but you're wrong. There are people out there who would pay for these images and pay well."

Tom nodded slowly. "Kaylan was part of it, he had to be," he said. "They both let Rico die. You can see that Kaylan looks dreadful, but he doesn't get any worse. He must have felt like shit, but he drank enough to stay alive."

Inigo Vitruvious and Kaylan Sully: two people who should never have met.

The noise of Charlie's phone shattered the silence.

"They were letting him go, on bail," Ravensbourne said without introduction. "But he's back in his cell, and I told his solicitor to fuck off and come back when we called. Forensics are coming to you, and uniforms to keep the place secure. I've sent the pictures to Hector Powell for his ideas. We need to know where those boys were kept and where Rico died. If they were kept in the college, it'll have to close while we search it. All of it."

"They weren't held here, boss," Charlie said.

"We'll talk about it when I get there," she said and ended the call.

"PLEASE, boss, just look. Close this block if you must, but not the whole college." Charlie didn't know when he'd become an advocate for Llanfair College of Art, only that he had. Without it the town would die like so many others, the young people leaving for Cardiff or England as the work dried up. The boost provided by the few hundred students wasn't much, but it was more than some other small towns had. He didn't want to see the beautiful building turned into flats, or more likely, left to rot, while councils, the Welsh Government and the National Lottery argued about what to do with it. Tom's tenure as college principal would end in scandal and failure. More to the point, he was sure Kaylan and Rico hadn't been kept there.

"Kaylan turned up at Brocklehurst Police Station," he said. "A few miles from where Vitruvious's father lives. Hayden James said the previous owner of his flat, who had a Vitruvious painting, moved to *somewhere near Manchester to be near family*. We should find out, at least. Vitruvious has one connection in the area, maybe more. No one would think to look for them near Brocklehurst, whereas people are coming and going here all the time."

Ravensbourne wasn't buying it; he could see that. "It had

to be somewhere he could keep them locked up, where they couldn't shout for help." Charlie was pleading now. "They would have been heard if they were here, and the Campus Services Officers have keys to every room."

"If you were me, Charlie," Ravensbourne said, "you would want every room in this place searched. Kaylan was found in Brocklehurst, but Rico was found here." She put a hand on his arm. "I'll get someone to talk to your Hayden, see if he knows any more about where this woman went, and we'll have a good look at Vitruvious's father, and his own house. But we're doing a proper search here, too."

In the end, it was Tom who provided the solution. "Next week is half term," he said. "We'll close early. Give everyone an extra couple of days off. Go through this place with a fine-tooth comb, Detective Chief Inspector. There will be no more cover-ups here."

Ravensbourne told Charlie to leave, and he went, though only on the promise of being included in the evening briefing.

Tom walked with him back to Dilys's. Their steps were slow, weariness dragging at their feet. The house was empty and quiet, with only the hum of the fridge to disturb the peace. Tom helped him up the steep stairs without asking, and then followed Charlie into the bedroom and closed the door. Dilys had made the bed and folded the dragon pyjamas on top of the duvet, waiting for Charlie's return. Except he wasn't the same person who had left the room this morning, and after what he had seen, he wasn't sure he ever would be.

"Do you need help to get changed?" Tom asked.

"What I need is for you to kiss me," Charlie answered, and put his arms around Tom's neck, feeling his beard against his own cheek as Tom kissed him and everything else was forgotten. It began gently, carefully, a kiss between two people who weren't quite sure of anything except a mutual attraction that had been building since that first encounter in the Rainbow. Charlie let all his insecurities go, and gave himself up to the moment, running his tongue over Tom's lips until they opened, and their tongues touched, sending sparks through Charlie's body. He felt the impact on Tom, too, and suddenly there was nothing tentative about this, no hesitation, just desire. Charlie broke the kiss.

"Too many clothes," he said, and got Tom's smile in return.

"Do you need my help?" Tom asked, and this time his tone was teasing.

"Yes, please," Charlie said.

He felt Tom's hands slide underneath his top and onto his skin and he shivered.

"Cold?" Tom asked.

"No, that's not it. In fact, if we both got naked, I think things would warm up very well."

Charlie did need help with his injured arm, but he managed the rest quickly enough to see Tom take his own shirt off. The tattoos covered both arms and shoulders with intricate patterns.

"They're your own drawings," Charlie exclaimed, and lay down on the bed, holding his arms out. He wanted to trace those lines with his fingers, and his tongue. Then Tom stripped off his trousers and underwear, and Charlie was distracted by the sight of Tom's erection. He sat up again, rolling onto his knees, and before Tom could move, took Tom's cock in his hand, easing the foreskin back, and then took it into his mouth, swirling his tongue around the head, tasting the saltiness of pre-come, and then taking him deeper until Tom groaned. He felt Tom's hands in his hair.

"Oh, fuck, Charlie," he said.

Yes please.

Charlie took Tom's cock deeper still, sucking, sliding his lips up and down, massaging Tom's balls with his hand, until Tom pulled away.

"I was enjoying that," Charlie said.

"Me too." Tom pushed him very carefully down onto the bed, being careful not to touch the dressings. "But now it's my turn." He knelt over Charlie and sucked each nipple in turn before running his tongue down Charlie's stomach over his hips and down the inside of his thighs and around his balls. Charlie's cock ached for attention, and he stroked himself.

"Come here," he said, "I need to kiss you again."

In reply, Tom rolled Charlie, very gently, onto his uninjured side and kissed him, long and deep, running his hand over Charlie's arse, between the cheeks and pressing the very tip of his finger into Charlie's hole. Charlie sighed. Their cocks touched, and Charlie moved closer, desire building.

"Don't stop."

"Stay there," Tom said. He got up and went to his suit jacket, producing a condom and a mini-packet of lube.

He slicked up his fingers, then lay on the bed and licked a stripe up Charlie's cock before taking him in his mouth without warning, making Charlie gasp with shock and pleasure. He gasped again when he felt a finger pressing into him, gentle, but insistent. Tom's beard nudged Charlie's balls, and the finger kept pressing in as Tom licked and sucked.

"Keep still," Tom said, pulling away, but Charlie couldn't. He felt a second finger, and it burned, but he didn't care because of Tom's lips and tongue.

"Oh, fuck," he groaned, "please, Tom."

Tom took no notice, just pressed his fingers in until he found Charlie's prostate and lit another flame. Ignoring the tearing sensation in his side, Charlie grabbed Tom's hair and pulled. His mouth slid off Charlie's cock, and he looked up, his lips swollen and saliva wetting his beard.

"Fuck me now," Charlie said.

"I'll hurt you."

"Not for long." Charlie rolled onto his elbows and knees, and if his ribs hurt, he decided not to feel them. He heard Tom with condom and lube, and then he felt what he wanted:

Tom's hands on his arse and Tom's cock at his entrance. It hurt, but not for long. Tom held his hips and slid in, a millimetre at a time until the burning settled.

"Move," Charlie said, and Tom did, slowly at first, until Charlie began to thrust backwards against him, wanting more, and harder. Charlie forgot everything except Tom's body against him, inside him, and the exquisite pleasure building and building. He cried out, calling Tom's name, as Tom drove into him, harder and faster, gripping Charlie's hips hard enough to leave bruises. And then he pulled out, ripped the condom off and pushed Charlie onto his back, leaning over him and taking both of their cocks in his hand. Charlie's hand joined Tom's and it took a few seconds of desperate thrusting before Charlie's orgasm rolled over him, wave after wave, and Tom followed, shouting as he came.

They lay together feeling the high, floating, despite the sweat and the stickiness, until the air chilled their skin, and the town hall clock struck two. The shower was barely big enough for one person, so they took turns, Tom helping Charlie to wash without wetting the dressings. Then they dried each other, climbed into bed and unexpectedly, slept.

30

Awake, again
THURSDAY 4.30PM

Charlie woke first, the little spoon against Tom's much bigger spoon. It felt comfortable, even with his sore ribs. Charlie could feel Tom breathing against him and thought he could drift off again if it wasn't for his need to know what, if anything, Ravensbourne had found. It was still light outside, and he struggled to look at the bedside table and his phone for the time. Only half past four. He could stay cuddled up to Tom for a bit longer. He could let himself imagine a repeat of sex with Tom, and more time spent listening to Tom talk about art. He still thought Tom was way out of his league, but a man could dream. And dream he did, feeling Tom's warmth against his skin, until he couldn't put off thinking about the murder, and the briefing for any longer.

Possibly no one would ever know whether Kaylan or Vitruvious had instigated the scheme, but both of them had deprived Rico of food and drink until he died. The pictures proved that Vitruvious at least, had done it knowingly.

Charlie looked at his phone again. It was coming up to five, and the briefing was at six. Would Dilys mind if he made some sandwiches? Probably not. He began to wriggle out from under the duvet, which was enough to wake Tom.

"Stay there," Charlie said, "I'm going to forage for a pot of tea and some sandwiches."

Tom smiled, as he always did, and sat up showing a chest covered with black hair, and those delicate tattoos covering both arms. Charlie still wanted to study them, but now wasn't the time.

"One-handed sandwich making?" Tom asked. "I don't think so. You stay here, and I'll go. You need to take your antibiotics, and I'll find some painkillers. Don't argue."

Charlie could have argued, but he decided not to. He ached, and the bed was soft and warm. Next time, if there was a next time, he could pay Tom back.

"Thank you," he said, "for everything."

Tom leaned over and kissed him. "Anytime," he said, as if he meant it.

FIVE MINUTES LATER, Charlie decided that crumbs in the bed was hardly fair on his landlady, even for the pleasure of another doze, so he got up and struggled into clean jeans, putting a hoodie round his neck for Tom to help him into. He walked barefoot into the kitchen to find Tom and Dilys assembling a tray of tea, sandwiches and cake. Dilys looked at his bandages with sympathy.

"Go in the lounge, sweethearts, and I'll bring the grub in," she said, and ignored the way Charlie blushed bright red. Tom followed him into the lounge and carefully helped him into the hoodie.

"Will you be warm enough?" he asked.

"I'll be fine," Charlie said, not knowing whether to object to the mollycoddling, or simply enjoy it. "We're meeting at the police station, and even the biggest room is tiny. I'm more likely to be too hot than too cold."

They drank tea and ate sandwiches and cake, Dilys joining them. It was peaceful and domestic, a far cry from the last few days. Could it be that the end of the nightmare of the last week was in sight?

As they finished eating, the front door opened and there was a cheerful cry of "Only me, Aunty D!" Eddy put his head round the door. He looked at Charlie. "Car's outside. Transport to the briefing for injured officers."

"Do you mind if I walk?" Charlie said. "Because it's less painful than bending over to get in a car."

"I'll walk round with you," Tom said, earning himself a nasty look from Eddy.

"Fine," Eddy said, and left without another word.

"Green-eyed monster?" Dilys asked. Tom went pink and Charlie shrugged. Then wished he hadn't as his ribs protested.

"It was thoughtful of him to come and see if I wanted a lift," Charlie said. "I'm sorry to upset him."

"He's a big boy," Dilys said, and started to clear the tea things.

Tom helped Charlie with his shoes and coat, and held him gently before they left the house.

"I don't want to kiss you in front of your colleagues," he said, "but I do want to kiss you. Afterwards I'd like to repeat my invitation to dinner."

"And etchings?" Charlie asked.

"Etchings can be provided."

The kiss was deep and tender, and if the circumstances had been different would probably have led back upstairs. But the circumstances were as they were.

They walked back towards the police station and parted when it came into sight.

"I'll ring you," Tom said.

Charlie hoped he would, that he wouldn't regret what had happened when he was back in his beautiful office and Charlie was back in his tatty police station.

. . .

HE WAS SURPRISED to see only Ravensbourne, Eddy and Patsy in the break room of the police station. They all had mugs of tea, and Patsy made one for him.

"We can't get any further tonight," Ravensbourne said. "But you need to know where we're up to. I should also tell you that I'm recommending the three of you, plus PC Jellicoe, for commendations for your work here." She put her hand up. "But that will take months. In the meantime, Gwilym Bowen has been charged with the assaults, and excellent news … forensics did a brilliant job on the van, Charlie's car, and the remains of a glass bottle. So, he's also going to be charged with the arson attack in the car park. He'll be going away for a few years at least."

"What about his bloody uncle?" Eddy asked.

"Resigned," Charlie said. "So, nothing, I guess."

"Look at it this way," Ravensbourne said. "He's gone from here. He's gone from Clwyd Police. Now there's one less of them. All we can hope for is to whittle away at the Masonic tendency. And his sergeant will be going too. So that's two fewer than yesterday."

Charlie felt a buzzing in his pocket. He slipped his phone out and checked it while Ravensbourne took a sip of her tea.

TOM PENNANT: *Missing you already, txt when you're done? X*

CHARLIE FELT HIS HEART JUMP. He hadn't let himself think Tom really did like him, but there was an x …

"Kaylan Sully's mother and father have arrived and have appointed a London solicitor. He's going *no comment* on everything. He can't deny shooting Charlie, or kidnapping Tom Pennant, but he's not giving an inch on anything else. Vitruvious is also going *no comment*, so he won't give us any evidence about today's events."

"But the drawings, boss."

"As you say, the drawings. You found them in Vitruvious's studio, but none of them are signed. There are people who may be prepared to testify that Vitruvious did those drawings, but unfortunately Kaylan Sully isn't one of them. For what it's worth, I think Vitruvious and Kaylan planned a series of pictures in which Rico died and Kaylan recovered, but proving it is a different thing. We haven't found where the young men were kept; only that it wasn't at the college. Don't worry, we're not going to give up. We've got warrants for Vitruvious's house, and for his father's house. We're looking at CCTV to see how Kaylan got to the Brocklehurst police station, and we're looking for the female relative who may or may not exist. Forensics are still working on the place Rico's body was found."

"But if Vitruvious keeps denying everything, he could get away with it." Charlie said, barely containing his fury.

"In the short term. Believe me, Charlie, no one who has seen those drawings is going to let this drop. And the Pepperdines are loaded. There will be big rewards. People's memories will be jogged. Someone will have seen something."

"Hey," Patsy said, "Kaylan is an arrogant shit who isn't going to like prison. My money is on him talking if it gets him out quicker. He hates Vitruvious enough to throw him under the bus."

"We have to rely on one psychopath to turn in another one. Fucking great." Charlie said. "And I suppose the money has all disappeared as well?"

"It has," Ravensbourne admitted. "But we can prove it was donated to the college, and I am sure as eggs is eggs that the Finance Director is going to cave in. He's the weakest link. He had to have helped siphon it off. Kaylan Sully might have stolen it, but there are some pretty skilled people on our side. They'll find it."

"Where does this leave us, boss?" Charlie asked.

"Tomorrow? Take a day off. People are used to the station being closed. On Monday, open the doors and start providing a service to the town. You need more people, and you'll get them. This building is a disgrace, and I'm talking to Estates about it. There's a PR job to be done in Llanfair, and I want you all here to spearhead it. I'm going to need Charlie to help with the interviews, and to carry on as the senior officer here"

Charlie had a lot of things he wanted to say, but Patsy got there first.

"So, what you're saying, ma'am, is that the corrupt police officers are getting off scot-free, and one of the murderers probably won't be prosecuted. The other murderer is only going to jail because he shot Charlie, and if that money is recovered it'll be a bloody miracle."

"Actually, it's probably worse than that," Ravensbourne said. "If Vitruvious isn't charged, he'll be free to go back to work."

They all contemplated this with downcast faces and heavy hearts.

"Tomorrow is another day," said Eddy. "We'll just have to find where the murder happened."

"And the police service in Llanfair is no longer corrupt," Patsy added. "The college has stopped covering things up, and no one can send dick-pics to our computers anymore."

They gathered up their coats and left the tea mugs in the sink. Ravensbourne rang her driver and promised to keep them posted.

Back out in the cold, Eddy locked the police station. Charlie stepped away from the others and got his phone out.

"I'm in the market for looking at etchings. Know anywhere I could find some?"

"I know just the place," Tom said. "I can't wait to show it to you. I'll pick you up in five minutes."

His heart did that little jump again.

I HOPE you enjoyed Charlie's first case in Llanfair. I hope you have enjoyed Charlie's latest book. If you have, I'd be delighted if you could leave a review on Amazon or Goodreads.

Charlie is back in Murder in Shades of Wood and Stone.

Want to know what happened...

To Charlie in Lanzarote?
Murder in Shades of Yellow
The full story - a novella, available now from Amazon in ebook and paperback.

Acknowledgments

Thanks are due to as always to Lou for daily 'nitting', and to Austin, who provided his usual encouragement. Big thanks to Bill, my inspiration, and without whom, none of this would be possible.

To real life Charlie, and to Glo, for giving me a break from the Author's Companion when those words just needed to be written.

To JL Merrow ... one day I will send you a clean manuscript.

Finally to the Author's Companion: stealer of pens and socks, shredder of cushions and chewer of shoes...sometimes all I need is to cuddle a dog.

About the Author

Ripley Hayes lives in rural Wales, where most of her stories are based, though she plays fast and loose with geography. She writes mysteries one reviewer has compared to Ruth Rendell; a compliment she hopes is justified. Her characters are usually gay, and they often have to solve their cases while dealing with the challenge that is life. Sometimes they fall in love.

She is frequently distracted by a certain dog, who likes to keep a poor author from getting too comfortable.

Her website is at ripleyhayes.com

You can find her on Facebook at Ripley and co.

Also by Ripley Hayes

Daniel Owen Books

DS Charlie Rees

Peter Tudor and Lorne Stewart Cosy Mysteries

Teema Crowe

Paul Qayf

Printed in Great Britain
by Amazon

40290547R00138